The NOT-SO-BORING Letters OF PRIVATE NOBODY

★ MATTHEW LANDIS ★

DIAL BOOKS FOR YOUNG READERS

DIAL BOOKS FOR YOUNG READERS
Penguin Young Readers Group
An imprint of Penguin Random House LLC
375 Hudson Street
New York, NY 10014

Printed in the United States of America
ISBN 9780735227989

1 3 5 7 9 10 8 6 4 2

Design by Mina Chung
Text set in Melior LT

TO HISTORY NERDS EVERYWHERE:
YOU ARE AWESOME.

CHAPTER ONE

THE PROJECT

Oliver knew Samantha wouldn't know.

He asked anyway.

"Did you know that Union General Ulysses S. Grant and Confederate General Robert E. Lee both went to West Point?"

Samantha whipped her dark hair back and copied down the homework posted on Mr. Carrow's PowerPoint slide. Oliver had already done that. He was always the first one to his table in social studies and always had the homework copied down before Mr. Carrow started the welcome music.

"No," she said.

"Grant was an average student, but crazy-good at riding horses. Lee graduated second in his class."

"I didn't know that either."

"And they both fought in the Mexican-American War."

"Really."

"Really. I mean think about that—two guys who went to the same military school and fought the same enemy fighting *each other* in the Civil War. How crazy is that?"

"Uh-huh."

Samantha swiveled around to talk with a girl at the next table. Oliver didn't really mind. Not everyone got how awesome the Civil War was, and that was okay. Awesome things still needed saying, and so he'd keep saying them.

"Grab a seat, gang," Mr. Carrow called over the indie rock music he blared pretty much every day. He was wearing a blazer, which meant they were starting a new unit.

"Lots to do, lots to do. So much that we probably won't even get started and you'll all fail the fourth marking period. Won't that be sad. Probably get some emails from parents. Not yours, Tara—they gave up on you long ago."

Laughter rippled through the class.

"But seriously, today is a big day. Maybe the biggest in your seventh-grade career. There is a small chance that you'll look back on this day and say, 'That was the greatest day of my life: the day we launched our study of the American Civil War.'"

Oliver pulsed with excitement. *Finally*. They were

going to study the thing he'd dedicated his life to. This was his arena—there was no chance of him not getting a hundred percent on this project. He would dominate and love every second of it.

"I promise that your Civil War experience will not be the one I had in seventh grade—memorizing endless battles, dates, and generals." Mr. Carrow's eyes swept past Oliver, landing for just a second. "Battles are important, and we'll study some of the big ones. And the generals who conducted the war were very interesting people, and we'll look at some of them too. But to really understand the impact of the conflict you need to look at the regular people—the soldiers, nurses, and slaves. You have to look at the mothers, daughters, and sons on the home front, and free African Americans in the North. What was the war like for them? The combined answer to *that* gives us a much better understanding of the war."

Oliver's grin turned into a flat stare. He couldn't really disagree with Mr. Carrow; the teacher was a master of history. Literally—he had a degree that said MASTER'S IN HISTORY. But Oliver didn't really get why he was downplaying battles, dates, and generals. Those things were what the war was made of. Oliver should know.

"Now: We've got a seasoned Civil War buff in our

midst—someone to fill us in when the textbook can't."
Mr. Carrow smiled at Oliver. "Ollie, I hope you can give
me some additional info when we dig into the battles."

"Uh, yeah." Oliver nodded. Okay. So all wasn't lost.

"Perfect. I want to lay out your unit project first.
This is the lens that we're going to use to view the
entire war." Mr. Carrow rapped his knuckles on a stack
of worksheets. "Table captains, come and get 'em."

Oliver basically ran up to the front table. He might
have shoved Ian out of the way. He handed the worksheets out to his table and speed-read the directions.

And he loved it all—almost. There was one issue: It
was a partner project.

But Oliver had found ways around that before. He
wasn't worried.

"Maggie, read the directions for us, would you?" Mr.
Carrow asked.

Maggie's straight black hair fell into her face as she
leaned toward the paper. *"With a partner, explore the
wartime experience of a Civil War contemporary. Your
goal is to answer a two-pr . . ."*

"Two-pronged," Mr. Carrow rescued.

"A two-pronged question: How did your character
impact the war, and how did the war impact your character?"

"Thanks Maggie, great job. Max, give us the formats."

Max unslouched a bit and started reading. *"You may present your findings in one of the following formats: documentary, PowerPoint, trifold, or dramatic presentation. For specifics on each format, consult the rubric on the back side."*

Oliver had already decided on a trifold. Of course he would do a trifold. Why *wouldn't* he do a trifold. He could fill it with tons of information and stand beside it dressed in his Civil War uniform. Maybe he could even bring his bayonet.

"Do we get to choose our partners?" asked Tommy.

"Let's vote on it," Mr. Carrow said. "Just kidding. This isn't a democracy—it's a somewhat benevolent dictatorship. Ian, I will define 'benevolent' for you after class. Dictator says, yes, you may choose your partners. But I reserve the right to reject any partnerships that could be harmful to your grade or my own sanity or both. You've got two minutes to figure that out. Go."

Oliver pretended not to hear the directions. While everyone else ran to a best friend or scavenged the wasteland of leftover partners, he stuck to his seat. He began to sketch the layout of his trifold.

"Oliver, over here." Mr. Carrow waved at him from a back table. "Need your help."

Yes. His abilities were already in demand.

Mr. Carrow motioned to the only student at the table.

She was Oliver's height but way skinnier. She was a beanstalk wearing too-big wrinkled jeans, a stained T-shirt, and a facial expression that wasn't exactly a frown but close enough. Thick brown hair that she never brushed hung in her eyes.

She was Ella Berry.

"I want you two to work together," Mr. Carrow said.

CHAPTER TWO

THE PARTNER

"I was going to work alone," Oliver said.

"You'll thank me once you realize how much work is involved. Grab your stuff and sit back here today. We're going to select our historical persons in a second and then do some brainstorming on formats."

Oliver had never talked back to a teacher. It wasn't in his DNA. He liked authority—it made the world organized and safe.

But a rebellion was stirring in his gut.

A secede-from-the-Union type of rebellion.

It wasn't really about Ella. Okay, it was kind of about Ella. Teachers always gave her quizzes back facedown— the universal sign of "You just totally and completely bombed this." There was a rumor she almost failed sixth grade. And that's what bothered Oliver: She had no dedication. He didn't care that she never talked and always looked like she'd climbed out of a dumpster. He was scared that she was going to mess up the project he'd been prepping for his entire life.

"Trust me on this one." Mr. Carrow clapped Oliver on the shoulder and left.

Oliver looked over at Ella.

Ella stared out the window.

"Behold: voices of the past." Mr. Carrow changed the PowerPoint to a slide of fifteen names. Oliver scanned them as he got his binder and rejoined Ella. Two big names popped out—Union General George McClellan and Confederate General Thomas "Stonewall" Jackson. Oliver knew all about them. He could give an oral report right now if he had to.

"Let's do one of the generals," he said to Ella. "Maybe Stonewall Jackson. I went to his shrine last summer in Virginia and took a bunch of pictures—"

"We're picking at random," Mr. Carrow announced. He held up the black top hat that he'd used to teach Lincoln's rise to fame (though technically, as Oliver had pointed out, Lincoln didn't wear that style hat until he was president). "I'll come by each partner group and one of you pick. Maggie, put a line through each name as it gets picked from the hat."

Oliver bounced his foot nervously as the first group reached into the hat. "I really hope we get a general," he said to Ella.

"Stonewall Jackson," Tommy shouted. "Sweet."

"Crap." Oliver glanced sideways at Ella. Still staring out the window. "There's one more general left. Don't give up hope."

Ella turned and looked at him. Her eyes reminded him of the water in those Caribbean getaway commercials. Green? Blue? It was hard to tell behind the wall of hair. She turned back to the window.

"Clara Barton to Sarah and Emily," Mr. Carrow proclaimed. Maggie ran a red digital pen through the famous nurse. Oliver could have done her too, but it wouldn't have been nearly as much fun since nurses didn't fight.

Mr. Carrow and the hat were getting closer to Oliver and Ella's table. About half the names were gone, with only one general left. Oliver prayed.

"Choose . . . wisely," Mr. Carrow said dramatically. Oliver bounced his foot harder. Mr. Carrow shook the hat, and the slips of paper rustled against one another. "Seriously—just pick one."

So Ella did.

CHAPTER THREE

THE PRIVATE

"*Private Raymond Stone*," Mr. Carrow read. "Oooo. That's a good one. Maggie, cross off Raymond Stone."

Oliver stared at the slip of paper in Ella's hand. She'd just reached in and grabbed it. Just like that.

"Who?" Oliver asked.

Ella looked closer at the slip of paper. She handed it to him.

"*Private Raymond Stone,*" Oliver read.

He tried to remain calm. He breathed in and out. But facts were facts: He'd been partnered with Ella for two minutes and she was already screwing things up.

"George Mc-McClellan?" Samantha stuttered as she read her slip. She and her partner both giggled. "Who's he?"

"He was the Union Army's commanding general for some of the war," Oliver answered automatically.

Samantha looked blank. He looked down at his slip. He looked at Ella. She peered back through her hair.

This was all falling apart quickly.

Oliver pulled out his phone and quickly googled "Private Raymond Stone."

He felt tricked. The Civil War was his thing, and in less than five minutes 1) he was forced into a partnership and 2) his partner picked a soldier that even Google had never heard of instead of a heroic general he already knew so much about.

Oliver put his phone away. Ella still hadn't said anything. It was getting awkward.

"Each of your historical persons—let's just call them 'HPs'—was an actual person who lived during the Civil War," Mr. Carrow explained. "Some survived, others didn't. I chose them specifically because they left behind a lot of information about their experience—military reports, letters, and diaries. Historians way more nerdy than me have digitized and transcribed them. These primary sources are all gathered on my website. They'll be your main focus."

Groans all around.

"Did it take me hours before and after school? Yes. I like Starbucks gift cards and cash. Don't underestimate end-of-the-year gifts. They can really help your project grade. Just kidding. But seriously: Tara, consider this a huge, obvious hint to get me something. You moving on to eighth grade depends on it."

Oliver shot up his hand. "Can we use other sources?"

"Such as?"

"Other books about the war we already own."

"Only to support your HP's account."

The rebellion was back in Oliver's gut. What about everything he already knew? Sure, some of it would come in handy—the basic stuff. But not the really interesting stuff that nobody but him knew about.

"Other questions? No? Okay. I want you to brainstorm with your partner about format. Choose one that's best for both of you. You got five minutes." Mr. Carrow plugged his iPhone back into the overhead speakers and turned the volume way down on his indie rock. "And I'd suggest exchanging phone numbers so you can coordinate who's doing what over the next three weeks."

–CHAPTER FOUR–
DOT-DOT-DOT

Ella's iPhone looked like one of the brand-new ones that cost six hundred dollars. It also had a big crack right down the screen. Oliver wondered why she didn't have a case on it, and if she realized the connection between the crack and the not having a case.

"Got it," he said when her cat emoji text came through on the ancient iPhone he'd inherited from his dad. Or maybe his dad's dad.

Oliver wasn't sure what to say next. He didn't have a whole lot of conversation experience. Mostly he just shared information with people, and most of that was about the Civil War.

"I don't get many texts, so I'll know right away if you message me. Mostly I just get texts from my mom. She always uses a lot of dot-dot-dots. I think she thinks you're supposed to text like you talk in real life, you know, like in big long sentences. Like this." He tilted the screen toward her. *"Oliver dot-dot-dot I am picking you up today at 9:30 for your dentist appointment dot-dot-dot please make sure to show Mrs. Mason your note so that she dismisses you to the office dot-dot-dot I will see you then dot-dot-dot please respond and let me know you got this dot-dot-dot."*

"Ellipsis," Ella said.

"What?"

"The dot-dot-dot thing. It's called an ellipsis."

"Oh." Oliver wondered how she knew that. He sat behind her in English and saw she'd tanked her *Outsiders* essay last week.

"My local historians," Mr. Carrow said, buzzing by their table. "You've hit the jackpot."

"How?" Oliver asked.

"Private Raymond Stone lived about five miles from this school."

Oliver waited for some other information that would make their pick a "jackpot."

"Come on, Ollie—this is good stuff. You two actually get to hold primary sources in your hands instead of just staring at a computer screen like everyone else." Mr. Carrow wrote a website on Ollie's paper. "Private Raymond Stone's great-great-somebody donated a bunch of family papers to a local historical society. You two can check them out whenever you want. S*he really* cool stuff there, I bet."

Oliver looked to Ella for confirmation t *this* sounded like the lamest thing ever.

She was busy sketching something on her pa

"So we're thinking trifold," Mr. Carrow said, g_ ing at Oliver's design. He looked at Ella's, which a bunch of squares covering the paper numbered 1 "Ah—a storyboard. Interesting. So you want to dc documentary?"

Ella shrugged.

Oliver panicked.

"We're doing a trifold," he told Mr. Carrow. "I've got it all planned. In the center—"

"Come on now—take a risk," Mr. Carrow said. He tapped Ella's storyboard. "I like this. Do you know how to use any editing software? Windows Movie Maker or iMovie?"

Ella shook her head.

"No worries. I can show you the basics, and YouTube will fill in the rest."

"Uh," Oliver said, "but I don't even know what kind of things go in a documentary."

"If only you had an amazing teacher who made a rubric with all the essential elements," Mr. Carrow said. He flipped over Oliver's paper. "O. M. G. It's a miracle."

He blocked the side of his face with one hand. "Please, no pictures."

Oliver frowned at the bullet point descriptions: a storyboard, a script, images, music, and voiceovers. And there was the issue of editing—which neither he nor Ella knew how to do.

"You've seen the PBS *Civil War* series by Ken Burns, right?" Mr. Carrow asked Oliver.

"Of course."

"Right. It's older, but a solid documentary example. Think about maybe borrowing a few of the techniques for your project. And again I'll refer you to YouTube for other examples." He surveyed them both, smiling like he was really proud of himself. "I think this is going to be a great partnership."

I think . . . you need your head examined, Oliver thought.

-CHAPTER FIVE-
THE FIRST MISTAKE

Oliver stared at his perfect ham sandwich. His mom made the best sandwiches.

But he couldn't eat. He was too upset.

Unfortunately, there was no one to tell because the only semi-normal kid at his lunch table—Kevin—was at a doctor's appointment. The rest of the kids were watching really confusing anime movies on their phones. Normally, Oliver would be reading one of his Time-Life Civil War books, but he wasn't in the mood.

He was in the mood to ask Mr. Carrow for a new group. A group of one.

A group of himself.

So back to Mr. Carrow's room he went.

"Hey buddy," Mr. Carrow said when Oliver came in. He forked fruit from a nearby bowl while his other hand scribbled on a stack of papers. "Leave something in here?"

"Uh, no." Oliver walked up to the desk. Out of nowhere he got a bad feeling about what he was about to say. But he had to ask anyway. Civil War greatness depended on it.

"I was wondering if I could work alone. For the project."

Mr. Carrow looked at him out of the corner of his eye. He scribbled a comment in the margin of a quiz. Oliver couldn't make it out. For a teacher, Mr. Carrow's handwriting was pretty bad. No, it was beyond bad. It was embarrassingly bad, actually, for any adult. Just awful. "Okay," he said, putting down the pen and giving Oliver his full attention. "Why do you want to work alone?"

"I just do."

"Why?"

The answer in Oliver's head went something like *Because my partner is ruining the project.* "Because I don't always get along with other students," he said instead.

"And you're worried that you won't get along with Ella."

"Uh-huh."

"You two seemed to be getting along today."

"I just want to work alone."

Mr. Carrow leaned back in his chair, fingers folded into a steeple. "What percentage of Civil War soldiers died from disease?"

"Close to seventy percent." Oliver had no idea how this was connected to his partner situation. "Why?"

"What's the range on a Civil War rifle?"

"About three hundred yards."

"What former Confederate city didn't celebrate Independence Day for almost eighty years because the citizens still hadn't gotten over their surrender to Union forces on July 4, 1863?"

"Vicksburg."

Mr. Carrow pounded a fist on the desk and laughed. "Ollie, look at this," he said, motioning to a poster hanging on the wall behind his desk. It was a photograph of General Ulysses S. Grant leaning against a tree. Oliver had always thought the man looked totally awesome in that shot. "You probably know more about this guy than I do. I really admire that. Your love of the Civil War gets me excited about it too."

"Uh, thanks," Oliver said. Still completely lost.

"What was Grant's life like, before the war?"

"One business failure after another," Oliver said. "He had to sell firewood on the streets of St. Louis just to feed his family."

"A decade later most of the country called him a hero; a few years after that they all called him Mr. President. Pretty crazy, right?"

"Uh-huh."

"Question is, how did those early struggles shape him as a leader? Things weren't always easy for him during the war, remember: some pretty costly battle blunders, a demotion, struggles with alcohol."

Oliver realized they were arriving at the point. He didn't like it. "I guess they made him a better commander. Taught him to stick with it, even when it was hard."

"Maybe he learned that difficulty precedes greatness."

"Yeah. Maybe."

"I'm going to copyright that. Steal it and I'll sue you into oblivion."

"So I can't work alone."

"Nope."

"Even if I'm pretty sure my partner will ruin the project."

Mr. Carrow didn't respond for a second. "That's a pretty bold statement, Ollie. I'd caution you to not judge people on a first impression."

Oliver felt horrible. "Okay. Can I have a pass back to lunch?"

Mr. Carrow scrawled on a Post-it note and handed it to Oliver. It looked like a three-year-old kid had tried to draw ancient runes. "Difficulty precedes greatness."

Oliver walked into the hall, wishing he hadn't come down. It had been pointless. And stupid. And wrong.

And when he saw Ella standing at her locker just a few feet from the door, and their eyes locked, those reasons slapped him, open-palm, directly in the face.

CHAPTER SIX

THE APOLOGY (ROUND ONE)

"Hey." It sounded so stupid, echoing in the empty hall.

Ella looked away. Had she overheard what he'd asked Mr. Carrow?

Of course she had; the door had been wide-freaking-open.

"So I was thinking—" Oliver started.

Students flooded the hall. Seventh-grade lunch was over and the sixth and eighth graders were changing classes. Oliver needed to get going, or he'd be late to fifth period.

But guilt forced him to weave through the crowd toward Ella. He had to make things right. "About the project—"

Ella shut her locker and walked into the stream of students.

The guilt formed an angry fist in Oliver's stomach during Spanish. By the end of gym, it was punching him repeatedly in the lungs. He couldn't remember feeling this awful. Was it possible to die of guilt?

"I need to go to Mrs. Mason's," Oliver told Mr. Carrow at Resource, their thirty-minute study period at the end of the day.

"Oliver, are you failing English?" Mr. Carrow asked.

"No."

"JK, Ollie. Got your team pass?" Oliver tapped the blue square on the front of his binder. "Boom. Sign out on the board so I know where you're at."

Oliver hurried down the hall, rehearsing his apology. *Ella: I'm sorry I asked to leave our group.* The fist of guilt pulverized a kidney. *I'm sorry I hurt your feelings. I'm looking forward to our partnership.*

Oliver walked into Mrs. Mason's room and halted. Twenty-six dead-silent students stared at him, including Kevin, Oliver's lunch buddy. He sat at Mrs. Mason's desk while she graded something he probably missed from being at the doctor's. He waved at Oliver like he was on the other side of a prison fence.

"What do you need, Oliver?" Mrs. Mason asked. Her pen found another mistake, bringing her one step closer to her life goal of making sure every seventh grader knew their writing was terrible. Her other life goals included having perfect hair and a cold stare that could turn you to stone.

So far she was winning at life.

"I'm here to see Ella."

Mrs. Mason cut short the ripple of "oooohs" with one swivel of her head. "About?"

"Our social studies project." Oliver spotted Ella in the back of the room doing her favorite thing: staring out the window.

"Good initiative." Mrs. Mason pointed to an empty table. "You two may work there."

Oliver sat down.

Ella didn't move.

Everyone stared.

"Ella?" Mrs. Mason asked. More window staring. Oliver's face tingled. This was getting embarrassing.

Ella picked up her binder and walked to the front of the room. She handed Mrs. Mason a yellow slip.

"Ella's leaving for an appointment, Oliver. Try again tomorrow."

"Uh. Okay." Oliver picked up his binder and walked out of the room. He could feel people staring at him as he went.

So he'd apologize tomorrow.

But then he turned around and saw Ella walking

toward the office. The fist of guilt jabbed his dia-phragm.

Run-walking down the hall behind her, Oliver dove right in. "I'm sorry I asked Mr. Carrow to leave our group. It was mean. I'm sorry." He finally caught up, scooted in front of her, and stuck out his hand. "I look forward to a productive partnership."

Ella brushed past him.

"Come on," he said, hurrying after her. "I'm really sorry. I don't know why I did it. Actually, that's not true. I know why. See, I really like the Civil War. My little sister says I'm obsessed. Anyway, I guess I got overprotective and felt like you were ruining the project—"

She stopped dead in her tracks. Oliver actually ran into her. She faced him.

"No—not that you *were* ruining it," he said. "But that's what I thought. You know, because you picked Private Stone. But you didn't really. I mean, you did pick him but it wasn't on purpose. This isn't coming out right. I think I'm making it worse. Am I making it worse?" He tried to find her eyes behind the hair for confirmation. Nothing. She started walking again, faster this time.

They had passed through the choking smog of the sixth-grade hallway, which always smelled like vanilla,

Axe body spray, and sweat. In a few steps they would turn the corner to the office. Oliver's blue team pass would be no good in these waters if he got questioned. He had to wrap this up fast.

"Nobody ever wants to work with me," he blurted out. "I'm pretty sure people think I'm weird. I don't know why. I guess I don't really know how to talk to people. I mean, *I* know how to talk, other people just don't listen. Is that mean? Oh jeez. This isn't coming out right." Ella rounded the corner. Oliver planted his feet inside students-allowed-with-a-pass territory and let his words carry down the short hallway. "I just really like the Civil War, okay? I love it. A lot. It's my thing, and I felt like you were kind of taking control of my thing. And that was hard for me. I'm sorry."

Ella stopped in front of the main office's glass doors. Oliver tried one last time: "Ella. I. Am. *Sorry!*"

She definitely wasn't listening. She was staring through the glass at a man and a woman, arguing. Both were dressed in expensive-looking clothes that Oliver figured all business people wore. Spotting Ella, they stopped fighting and waved like everything was fine. Both of them looked tired.

Ella turned around and looked at Oliver for a few seconds. "Okay."

The fist of guilt ceased its merciless punching. "Okay?"

"Okay." Ella opened the office door and walked inside.

And then she and her parents walked into the conference room attached to Principal Fastbender's office.

CHAPTER SEVEN

THE MANY TERRIFYING CONFESSIONS OF ELLA BERRY

"Grab a seat next to your partner and log on," Mr. Carrow said two days later as third-period social studies trailed into the computer lab. "Once you're on, go to my website. If you forgot the address, ask someone other than me because asking me will result in a very sarcastic response such as, 'You forgot the website we've been using all year? The website that literally contains my first initial and last name?'"

Oliver hadn't talked to Ella since their "Okay okay okay" moment. He wasn't ignoring her, he just wasn't sure what to say. It was like they were sitting on opposite ends of a seesaw: He didn't know if she wanted to actually interact on the thing, so he'd just planted his feet to keep it balanced.

"Hey," Oliver said.

Ella slid into the chair next to him and turned on

the computer. Another ratty T-shirt and pair of too-big jeans. Hair like she'd been fighting off bees.

"Hey," she said back.

At least the seesaw was moving.

"Today's goal is simple," Mr. Carrow said. "I want you to start digging up the basic biographical info on your HP using the links I provided." He held up a worksheet. "This is where you'll begin listing the information you find. Some of the documents have hard facts, like town or church registries that list births, marriages, and deaths; others might focus on the big picture, like letters home from the battlefield. Every source tells us *something* that's critical to understanding your HP and their experience during the war." He looked at the clock. "Hands up for questions, I'll be buzzing around. Fifty minutes, gang. Don't waste it."

Oliver went up and got their worksheets. "I picked these computers because they're the fastest," he said, giving Ella a sheet. "And because they're the farthest from the teacher's desk in the back. You know why it's in the back? So they can watch our screens. But I found out that the distance and glare from the ceiling lights make our screens basically impossible to read. One time I watched this History Channel video during Tech and no one noticed."

Why couldn't he just stop talking?

Ella opened up a browser and clicked around. "Fastbender told my parents I'm in danger of failing the year. That's what that meeting was about."

Oliver swiveled his head and stared at her.

"What?" Ella asked.

"Uh, nothing. Just . . . you haven't said much, and then you kind of just dropped an information atom bomb on me."

"I say things when they need to be said."

"Oh. Okay." Oliver paused. "What subjects are you failing?"

"Most of them." Ella didn't sound happy or sad. She wasn't bragging either. It was more like a statement of the facts—an observation, really.

A small fire of injustice flared in Oliver's chest. This was exactly why he'd asked to work alone. Ella obviously didn't care about her grades, so she obviously wouldn't care about the Civil War. She was going to sink the project. This was a giant catastrophe.

"So what happened, at the meeting?" Oliver asked.

"Fastbender said I have to get a D in this class if I want to move on to eighth grade."

"A *D*? What do you have now?"

"An F."

The small fire of injustice roared to a forest fire of fury. "How low of an F?"

"Forty-two percent."

"Sweet Moses." It was a phrase Oliver's mom said when something really shocked her. He didn't really know what it meant, other than that someone had just said something horribly shocking. "There's only two big assessments left in the marking period—this project and the Civil War unit test."

"I know."

"What grade do you—"

"I have to get hundreds on both."

"Mary, Mother of all that is holy." He'd heard his dad whisper that only once: when his little sister, Addie, had drawn stick figures all over their white couch with a Sharpie.

Now felt just as appropriate.

"I can fail two classes and still move on to eighth grade," Ella said, unfazed by Oliver's reaction. "English and math are low F's—really low—but social studies is salvageable." She did a quick calculation in the air with an index finger. "If I keep science and French at steady C's, then a perfect score on this project will bring social studies to a D. I'll pass. Barely."

The strangest part about the last three minutes—

aside from Ella detailing a master plan to *barely* pass seventh grade—was that she'd somehow been reading her screen the entire time.

"What's that?" Oliver asked, nodding toward her computer.

"It's the historical society website. They have a little paragraph about our soldier Private Stone, but we'll need to go there in person to see the whole collection of letters and stuff."

"What's happening right now?"

"What do you mean?"

"This." He tapped her screen. He tapped her paper. He tapped the screen again. "You're on task. Actually, you're ahead of task."

"I told you. I need a perfect score on this project."

"I don't get it."

"Get what?"

Oliver wasn't sure how she didn't get what he didn't get. "Why are you working so hard to get the lowest passing grades possible?"

Ella turned and looked at him like she had outside the main office two days ago. Like she was inspecting him.

But this time he failed whatever test she thought made him deserve a real answer.

"Just because." Ella went back to her screen and

ran a finger along the words. "Okay. Raymond Stone was born in Doylestown, Bucks County, Pennsylvania in 1842 to William and Eliza . . . had a sister named Rachel . . . his family owned a wheat farm."

Oliver jotted down the boring facts. "Looks like we're off to an exciting start."

"In September of 1862 he enlisted with the 68th Pennsylvania Regiment in Philadelphia and died on July 5, 1863 at Gettysburg of dysentery. What's that?"

"It's basically diarrhea," Oliver said. How heroic. Killed by his own poop.

Oliver stopped writing. "Wait—the 68th? That's wrong. He would've enlisted in the 104th."

"How do you know that?"

"Because"—Oliver puffed out his chest a little— "that's my reenactment regiment, the 104th Pennsylvania Volunteers—based on the actual regiment raised from our town. Soldiers joined local regiments, so Stone couldn't have been in the 68th way down in Philly. He would have enlisted in the 104th."

"That's not what the website says."

"Then the website is wrong."

Ella shrugged. "Then I guess you can tell that to the historical society people when we see them on Friday."

Oliver sighed, but it came out more like an *ugh*.

And then he *ugh*ed again.

CHAPTER EIGHT

THE UNINVITED LUNCH GUEST

"You're acting weird," Kevin said. He forked kimchi into his mouth and raised one eyebrow at Oliver.

"What do you mean?" Oliver asked.

"You're staring at your food instead of eating it."

"I'm thinking."

"About what?"

Oliver filled him in on the Ella situation.

"That's weird," Kevin announced without taking his eyes off his phone. "Really weird."

"I know," Oliver agreed. Kevin was basically the closest Oliver had to a friend. They ate lunch together every day. Well, not really together—Ollie was usually examining an epic battle, and Kevin was usually checking the comments on one of his weird Wattpad stories—but at least across from each other.

"Check it out." Kevin flashed his screen. "Remember

that Wattpad story I wrote last week, 'The Tyrannical Toothbrush'? It's up to three hundred reads and forty-seven stars."

"Nice," Oliver said. "Which one was that?"

"A power-hungry toothbrush launches a bathroom coup and institutes a rather harsh social order based upon each tool's perceived usefulness."

"Right."

All of Kevin's stories were kind of like that: incredibly strange.

"I think there's a story in your situation," Kevin said. He air-typed for a couple seconds. "How's this: It's the year 2090 and the world is on the brink of nuclear war. To keep the peace, the United Nations creates a fight-to-the-death tournament where the winner gets to blow up whatever country they want. China wins because of martial arts and stuff, but before the missiles launch, this thirteen-year-old American girl, who everyone thought was really stupid because she almost failed middle school, hacks into the system and makes the missiles blow up over the ocean."

"Sounds pretty weird."

Maybe it hadn't been such a good idea to try and talk to Kevin. Oliver reached for his book.

"Hey." Ella put her cafeteria tray down next to Oliver. He looked up at her in surprise, but she started talking, like she belonged right there at their table. "I was thinking we should start learning about Windows Movie Maker after school today."

"Windows Movie Maker sucks," Kevin said.

"It does?" Ella did a quick head-whipping motion to clear the tangled hair from her mouth before shoving in a chicken sandwich. Oliver watched it disappear in three bites. It was extremely impressive.

"It's the worst editing software ever created." Kevin glanced up, like he'd just noticed someone new was there. "Oh—we were just talking about you. I'm using your plan to almost fail seventh grade as a template for a short story. The working title is 'The Reluctant Hacker.' Don't worry—I won't use your real name."

"You were talking about me?"

"Uh," Oliver said, "I just filled Kevin in a little—about why we need to get a perfect score."

Ella shrugged. She unwrapped her second sandwich and crunched the tinfoil into a tiny ball. "What about iMovie? Mr. Carrow brought that up too."

"Yeah, iMovie is good," Kevin said. "Do you have a Mac?"

Ella nodded. Her cheeks were too packed with chicken to speak.

"Then you're good to go."

She swallowed and looked at Oliver. "Are you in the play?"

"No."

"Jazz band?"

"No."

"Baseball?"

"I'm not a ball sports kind of person."

"So can we go to your house after school?"

"Uh . . . Okay."

"Do you walk or ride?"

"Walk."

"All right." Ella stabbed seven tater tots onto a fork and shoved them into her mouth. "Let's meet at the bus loop."

"Uh . . . Okay."

"Romance," Kevin said. He darted his eyes between them. "The story needs romance. How about this: The tournament champion is secretly in love with Ella's mom, who's from America. He can't lose the tournament because the Chinese government will kill his family. But if he wins, they'll nuke his girlfriend. Now that adds some tension."

Ella studied the peas dying of dehydration on her tray. She did not pick up her fork. "What are you going to change my name to?"

"How do you feel about Cleopatra?"

"Sure." Ella looked over at Oliver's unopened pack of Tastykake Butterscotch Krimpets. "Are you going to eat those?"

". . . No."

"Can I have them?"

Oliver passed them to her. "Did you skip breakfast or something?"

"No."

Oliver watched her down a Krimpet in a single bite. "Do you always eat this much?"

"Yeah." She must have read his mind, because she added, "My parents are obsessed with gluten-free, sugar-free, taste-free stuff. Plus I have a high metabolism."

"My mom says I have the metabolism of a Peruvian weasel," Kevin said. "I looked it up—doesn't exist. But it made for a good story called 'The Peruvian Weasel' where a young weasel is taken hostage by a clan of gophers and brought to Patagonia. He works in a mining camp, escapes during an earthquake, and makes his way back to Peru to find out his wife remarried and his kids hate him. It's got over four hundred likes on Wattpad."

"Sounds cool," Ella said.

Kevin examined Ella over his phone. "Yeah—it is cool. Now if you can get Mrs. Mason to agree, I don't have to spend any more Resource choking on her old-lady perfume."

"Is that why you were at her desk on Monday?" Oliver asked. It felt weird asking Kevin about something that mattered. But whatever. Ella had started it.

"Yeah. I was trying to get some extra credit by showing her my Wattpad stuff. But *she* said it doesn't 'align with the school curriculum'"—he air-quoted this part—"and so I'm stuck doing these horrible argument-writing exercises with her twice a week. It's as awful as it sounds."

The hulking guidance counselor who babysat seventh-grade lunch announced over the mic that it was time to clean up.

"Meet you in the bus loop," Ella said, picking up her tray and leaving.

"Uh, okay." Oliver watched her go, wondering how in the world he'd arrived at this moment.

"She's not that weird," Kevin said.

Oliver looked at him. "Are you serious?"

"I thought she was cool."

CHAPTER NINE

THE FIRST GIRL TO ENTER OLIVER'S ROOM OTHER THAN HIS MOM AND SISTER AND COUSIN NATALIE

Oliver squinted in the blazing afternoon sun as he and Ella cut across the baseball outfield toward his subdivision. Some construction guys were taking down the giant WELLER GROUP, INC. sign that had been up during the school's two-year renovation (which for some reason hadn't involved putting in air-conditioning). Some hilarious person had spray-painted streamers and a string on the company's red diamond logo so it looked like a kite.

It was humid. Oliver was sweating. He was also scrambling to get a grip on this rapidly evolving situation. He didn't have friends over, ever. Which made having a girl over even stranger.

"So I have a sister," Oliver said. "Addie. She's in fifth grade. She's probably going to annoy you because that's her second-best skill. Her best skill is playing the piano. Her teacher has these recitals all the time and they're like the worst way to spend a Sunday afternoon. I've tried a thousand things to get out of them but nothing ever works. My parents say that families are supposed to support each other. I get it, but the recitals are still terrible."

They reached the tree line and Oliver led the way down a narrow dirt path that dumped them in between two backyards. At the sidewalk they turned left and walked down the street that ended at Oliver's house.

"Do you have any brothers or sisters?" he asked.

"A sister, but she's older."

"Like, high school?"

"College."

"Oh. That's cool. Does she drive you around and stuff when she's home?"

"She's usually busy."

At the stop sign they crossed the street to Oliver's driveway with the old silver minivan parked right in the middle. It was easy to spot because of the oldness, but also because of the two rear-window stickers: a giant keyboard on one side, and a cartoon Civil War soldier on the other, above the caption WORKING IS FOR PEOPLE WHO DON'T REENACT THE CIVIL WAR.

"Just to warn you," Oliver said as he punched in the garage code, "my mom might act funny. I actually have no idea what to expect. Not because of you." Oliver stopped at the mudroom door. "It's just that I don't have friends come over a lot."

"What about Kevin?"

"Kevin doesn't come over."

"But you guys are friends."

"Uh, I guess."

"You sit together at lunch."

"I know. The point is, just don't worry about my mom. She's really nice, but super nosy and up in my business lately. Sometimes she forgets I'm not in Addie's grade."

They went through the mudroom and into the kitchen. A bowl of Cheez-Its and a plate of sliced apples sat on the breakfast bar next to a Capri Sun pouch.

"What's this?" Ella asked.

Oliver wasn't exactly sure what she was asking. "After-school snack."

"Is it always like this?"

"Um, sometimes we have trail mix."

"Can I have some?"

"Sure." Oliver got another Capri Sun and they sat on opposite sides of the counter eating snacks. Ella ate more than eighty percent of the food.

"So this is ready for you every day when you come home?" she asked.

"Yeah."

"That's pretty cool."

"Uh, I guess."

"*Consider yourself—at home!*" sang Oliver's mom. "*Consider yourself one of the—*" She danced into the kitchen still wearing her blinding orange Home Depot apron. "Oh—hi."

"Mom, this is Ella."

"Ellaaaa," Oliver's mom said, like Oliver had brought home a long-lost relative. "Ella . . . nice to meet you."

"Thanks for having me, Mrs. Prichard." Ella stood up and shook Oliver's mom's hand. "I hope you don't mind that I invited myself over. We have to work on a project."

"Mind?" She laughed. "Of course not, honey." Her eyes darted between Oliver and Ella. Her smile was downright sinister. "No—no, I don't mind."

"And thanks for these snacks. I was starving."

"Then let me get some more." She went to the pantry and took out the Costco-size bag of Cheez-Its. She was wearing a ridiculous smile and kept stealing glances at Ella, like she was trying to make sure she was actually there. Oliver wanted to crawl into the dishwasher. "Oliver, you didn't mention a project. What's it about?"

"The Civil War," Ella answered.

"Oh! Ollie loves the Civil War!"

She put the new bowl of Cheez-Its down right in front of Ella.

"Thank you, Mrs. Prichard."

"Call me Mrs. P, honey," she said.

"Okay. Thanks, Mrs. P."

"We should get started," Oliver said, grabbing his book bag. It was time to get out of there, before his mom and Ella got too chummy. He headed for the basement—his room. Ella grabbed the bowl of Cheez-Its and followed him.

Oliver flicked the switch at the top of the stairs and took his time on each step. He was nervous. Why? Because the basement was his Civil War man cave? No. That was something to brag about. It was something else.

"This is my room," he told her. "I don't usually have people down here. Definitely not girls. You're the first, actually, other than my mom or sister. And my cousin Natalie. Last Christmas she drank the adult eggnog and got really sleepy."

Ella put her book bag on the couch Oliver's uncle had given him when they'd moved. "Wow," she said. "This is really awesome."

Other hand-me-down furniture filled the finished basement: A coffee table and TV from an aunt formed a sort of living room area. Bookshelves that G-Pop built took up most of the back wall, along with a giant wooden desk—also built by G-Pop—which was hilariously large and dangerously heavy.

"Where did you get all these flags?" Ella asked, examining the Civil War regimental flags hung like wallpaper.

"eBay. There's a lot of Civil War people on eBay."

"You really like the Civil War."

"Uh-huh."

"Why?"

Oliver looked at her sideways. Nobody had ever asked him *that* before. He thought for a beat.

"I like that it's infinite."

"Like, big?"

"Yeah." He'd never said this out loud. "It's like a giant mountain of information. Most people can see the famous peaks, but only from a distance. Climbing it is a lot different. When you're on the mountain you learn all sorts of really interesting stuff that other people don't know."

"That's a really good metaphor," she said. "Give me an example."

Was she messing with him? Oliver watched her for a second. Her face looked totally genuine. He relaxed.

"Okay. So you know General William T. Sherman— the guy famous for ending the war sooner by marching through the South and basically burning everything in sight? He was bipolar—like he had really, really bad depression. So bad that he was actually relieved of command during the first year of the war. His wife nursed him back to health with food and Shakespeare, and he returned to the army six months later."

"I didn't know that," Ella said. He could tell from her voice that she was thinking about it and actually interested—that she didn't just want him to shut up. "You wouldn't expect that, for someone who went on to do something so important in the war."

"*I know,*" Oliver said. "I mean, how cool is that? That somebody who was such a train wreck wound up ending the bloodiest war we've ever fought?"

"It's like the war is full of secrets or something." Her eyes wandered to the farthest corner of the basement. "Why do you have a bunk bed?"

"Uh, Addie and I shared a room in our other house. It was really small." Oliver pointed to the door beside it. "There's a bathroom, there, if you need."

"How long have you lived down here?"

"Since last year when Addie started getting serious about piano. It gets really loud." He put his hand awkwardly on the TV. Was he supposed to sit on the couch? His bed? No, not the bed. Yikes. He didn't know much about having a girl in his room, but that seemed like the opposite of a good idea. And anyway, which bunk—top or bottom?

Ella solved things by sitting on the couch and opening her MacBook on the coffee table. "Okay, YouTube. Teach me iMovie."

Oliver sat. Not too close. Probably too far. Was it weird to scoot closer? Who knew these things.

By the time Addie stomped into the house an hour later and started banging out scales on the piano, they'd covered the video editing basics. Music was a cinch too; the hardest part was finding a website to convert a YouTube music video to an audio file without also downloading a ton of spyware.

"She's pretty good," Ella said. Addie had finished her warm-up scales and moved on to a song so annoyingly familiar that Oliver sometimes hummed along by accident.

"She practices a lot."

"Wanna try making something with actual footage?"

"Sure."

Ella took out her iPhone and connected it to the MacBook with a white cord. "I've got some footage we can use."

She imported it and pressed PLAY.

It was a video of an open hand holding a playing card—a queen of diamonds. The hand was up close, really *really* close to the camera. It was Ella's hand, Oliver figured, because in the background was a fluffy bed and some posters on the wall.

"So what am I looking at?" Oliver asked. He didn't get it. The video hand was moving a tiny bit, up and down in a rhythm, almost like a handshake.

And then the card disappeared.

"What the—"

Oliver pushed his face closer to the computer.

"What just happened?"

Behind her tangled hair, Ella snorted.

CHAPTER TEN

THE GIRL WHO DOES MAGIC
AND LISTENS TO MOZART

"What just happened?" he asked again.

Ella laughed. "It's a magic trick."

"You edited the footage already," Oliver said. "You're messing with me."

There was no other possible explanation.

He grabbed the mouse and dragged the playhead back to the beginning and pressed the space bar. He watched the card disappear again.

"How did you do that?"

"I practiced. A lot."

"Show me."

Ella reached in her bag and took out a worn deck. "It's better on camera because you can't see the trick of it."

Taking a card at random, Ella sat on the coffee table so her hand faced Oliver like on the video. She relaxed her wrist, then began moving it up and down. "Moving my arm helps distract your eye from when the card disappears. That's what the guy in the YouTube video says, anyway."

Suddenly, there was a flash of the white card. And it was gone.

Ella waved her palm gently for a second or two, and then the card reappeared.

"HOLY! CRAP!" Oliver yelled. He stood up. He laughed. "That is the greatest thing I've ever seen."

Twelve more times Oliver watched her do the disappearing/reappearing trick. Each time it got better, and each time her smile widened until it took over her face. Obviously Oliver knew the card was hiding behind her palm, but that wasn't the point. The trick was super simple, but super deceptive.

"That is *the coolest* thing I have ever seen," he told her for the hundredth time. "I'm serious. Ella. That's amazing. Are you allowed to tell me how you do it? Or is there a magician code or something?"

"It's right here the whole time," she said, doing the trick and then flipping her hand over to show him. She grinned. "Then you just bring it back."

"Everything okay?" his mom called down.

"Mom," Oliver yelled back. The piano had stopped too. "Come down here. You have to see this."

"See what?" Addie called out. She tromped over-head and then down the steps, her bushy red pony-tail bouncing the whole way, with their mom trailing behind.

"Watch this," Oliver said. "It's a card trick. Watch."

Ella did the trick—her best one yet.

"It's behind her hand," Addie said. It was more like an accusation, really. She pushed past Oliver to see for herself, but Ella had already turned her hand over sheepishly.

"Yeah," Ella said. She wasn't smiling anymore. "You just flick it back real quick. It's not really that good."

"I think it's great," said Oliver's mom. "Very clever."

"Hmm," Addie said. She smoothed her blue jumper out and looked Ella up and down. "What's your name?"

"Ella."

Oliver was realizing this might not have been the best idea—holding a giant reunion of all the girls who had been in his room, cousin Natalie aside. "Okay, we have to get back to work," he said.

"Why is your hair so messy?"

"Addie!" Oliver's mom said sharply. "That is very rude. Upstairs."

Addie's ears went pink, like they always did when she was in trouble and about to fake-cry her way out of it. "Sorry," she mumbled, tromping back up.

"Ella, I'm very sorry," Oliver's mom said. "She knows better."

Ella twirled some tangled hair between her fingers. "It's okay."

"Oliver's dad will be home in about twenty minutes. If you like tacos, I can make it up to you."

"I like tacos," Ella said.

Oliver's mom looked pleased and relieved. "Good. Do you have to call your parents and let them know?"

"I'll text them."

Twenty minutes later they were sitting at the kitchen table building tacos. Oliver's parents sat on the short ends, with Oliver and Ella on one long side and Addie on the other. She was doing that "pity me" routine that she always did after being lectured—like it was Oliver's mom who had done something wrong.

"So, Ella," Oliver's dad said as he loaded his taco with meat. Oliver figured that as someone who sold meat for a living, he should know there's no way he was going to be able to fit all that ground beef in the taco and still have a chance of closing it. "Are you a Civil War nerd too?"

Ella's mouth was full of taco. She chewed for an awkward eternity before answering.

"No. But I'm learning to like it more than I did before."

"Ollie's obsessed with the Civil War," Addie declared. Her mom raised a warning eyebrow. "What? It's *true.*"

"I heard your scales today," Oliver said. "They were pretty bad."

Oliver's mom turned and gave him the Look. "My scales weren't bad," Addie protested.

"Your B-flat was."

"It's the hardest one."

Oliver was being a little meaner than usual, and it felt good. A little like he was protecting Ella—like he was getting back at Addie for what she'd said about Ella's hair.

Yeah. That was it.

And it felt like the most perfectly right thing to do.

"Someone who practices as much as you do should have it down already," Oliver said.

"That's enough," his mom said.

Oliver turned away from Addie. "We're making a documentary," he told his dad. "It's about some Union private named Raymond Stone. Every group got assigned a historical person who was alive during the war, and we got him. We're supposed to research his life and find out how the war impacted him."

"And how he impacted the war," added Ella.

"You were playing cards when I went down," Addie muttered.

"It was a card *trick*—a really good one. And it's way cooler than banging out some boring song in a way that would embarrass the guy who wrote it."

The burst of anger surprised Oliver. He was out for blood. His sister looked shocked.

"Son," Oliver's dad said in a *stop it right now or else* voice.

"Sorry, Addie," Oliver mumbled. She was actually hurt. Maybe it was time to back off—Ella didn't need this much protecting.

"I liked your song," Ella said, breaking the tension. "Fantasy in D Minor, right?"

Addie blinked at her. "You know *Mozart*?"

"A little."

"Do you *play*?"

"No, just listen. Is Mozart your favorite?"

Addie shifted to her knees and pushed her elbows on the table. "No—Bach is my favorite. I really want to play Andante—have you heard of it? It's for my next recital but my teacher says I'm not ready. It goes like this—"

She started humming the piece. Oliver dreaded sitting through the whole thing at some future recital.

"I hope you get to learn it soon," Ella said. "It sounds very pretty."

Addie beamed. She looked around the table and shoved a bowl of sour cream toward Ella like a thank-you gift. "Me too. *Me too.*"

The house line rang, but Oliver's parents let it go to the machine. They always said only credit card companies call during dinner time.

"Mrs. Prichard," came a hurried voice after the answering machine beep, *"this is Denise Fastbender, Principal of Kennesaw Middle Sch—"*

Oliver froze as his mom rushed to the phone. "Hello, hello—Mrs. Fastbender, this is Camille, Oliver's mom. Is everything all right?"

Ella set her fork down. Oliver saw her check her phone under the table. His stomach churned. Definitely too much taco in there for something like this.

"Uh, yes—yes, she's here. They've been working on a social studies project." Silence. Nodding by Oliver's mom. He saw that look of flashing worry fade to calm but concerned. "Yes, okay. I understand. Do you have our address to give them? Okay. Great. I apologize for the confusion, I thought she'd told them she would be here." Silence, more nodding. "Okay. You too, and again we're very sorry. I'm glad it's all sorted out. Good night."

She hung up and gave Oliver's dad one of those looks.

"Addie, come help me work on my B-flat scale," he said. Addie looked from Ollie to Ella, eyes wide, then followed her dad to the piano.

"Ella," Oliver's mom said. "That was Mrs. Fastbender. She said your parents have been trying to get a hold of you for over an hour. Didn't you tell them you were here?"

Ella stared at her food. "I'm sorry, Mrs. P. I guess my text never went through."

Oliver couldn't stand watching her squirm. "Sometimes that happens, remember?" he lied. "Bad reception in the basement."

"Hmm," Oliver's mom said. He wasn't sure if she bought it. "Your mom is on her way over and I'm sure she's relieved. Why don't you go get your stuff?"

Oliver paced around the foyer as Ella got her computer and book bag. His mom watched the driveway. Dad butchered scales while Addie corrected him.

"That's them," Oliver's mom said.

Oliver peeked out the window and saw a sparkly white SUV pull into the driveway. It made the Prichard family van look even crappier. Ella's mom stepped out wearing fancy business clothes and high heels.

"Sorry again, Mrs. P," Ella said as Oliver's mom opened the door.

"It's okay, honey. I'll walk out with you."

"Bye, Ollie."

In the driveway, the parents talked. Oliver saw lots of apologetic hand motions from his mom and lots of worried ones from Ella's. Ella's mom hugged her, but she just stood there and took it. It was all kind of off—forced. He wasn't sure why Ella had lied about texting her mom.

All he knew was that she wasn't the girl he'd thought she was.

She was the girl who did magic tricks and listened to Mozart.

Who knew.

CHAPTER ELEVEN

THE FRIEND

Oliver wasn't sure where to start, so he just went for it.

"Why don't we ever hang out?"

"We're hanging out right now," Kevin said without looking up from his phone.

"I mean at each other's houses. Play video games and stuff. Go to the movies."

"My parents think movies are too expensive. We Redbox. And you said you hate video games."

"You know what I mean." Oliver picked at his Cheez-Its. He thought about Ella, and how she would've annihilated the entire bag already.

"Are we friends?" Oliver asked.

"What do you mean?"

"I don't know." Oliver really didn't. "Are we . . . you know—friends."

Kevin put down his phone and shoveled in a big

bite of beef bulgogi. "Yeah. Maybe not good friends, but we're not *not* friends."

"Oh." Well, that settled it. "Okay."

"I never thought you wanted to be *good* friends."

"What?"

"You never ask me to hang out on the weekends. You never text, except for that one time by accident. And whenever we talk—which is only at lunch—you only talk about the Civil War."

"Uh, yeah, but—"

"It's okay," Kevin said. "I'm just telling you what it's like from my side of the table."

"You never ask me to hang out either."

"That's 'cause you're always telling me about some reenactment you're doing and how it's much more awesome than anything else in the world, ever."

"Yeah, but you don't talk about anything but your Wattpad stories."

"If I didn't, we'd only ever talk about the Civil War."

They traded blank stares.

"This is weird," Oliver said.

Kevin looked at the other kids at their table, lost in their anime movies and fantasy books. One kid was doing three Rubik's Cubes at a time. "Compared to what?"

Oliver laughed.

"What made you think about this?" Kevin asked, back on his phone.

Oliver shifted his eyes around the room. He'd never noticed where Ella sat before, and wasn't really sure where to look. "You know that girl, Ella? She was at my house a couple days ago, working on Mr. Carrow's social studies project. She asked if you and me were friends."

"What'd you tell her?"

"I said no."

"That's fair. What's her deal, anyway?"

"I actually have no clue." There—on the outdoor patio, Oliver spotted her. Sitting at a shaded picnic table with some girls, earbuds in. Probably eating triple her weight in chicken patties. "She's not dumb, but she's failing; her parents are rich—you should have seen her mom's car—but she's a mess."

"She's skinny but eats like someone who just got off a desert island," Kevin said. "And she's pretty, but she looks like she gets to school via tornado."

Oliver wasn't sure where he settled on that pretty point. "I think the hair's got something to do with her mom."

"You should ask her."

"I did. She wouldn't tell me."

Kevin made a *what do you want from me here?* face and took a swig of Gatorade.

Oliver stomped back and forth over these questions in his head for a minute. "She can do this really amazing card—"

"Friends don't always talk, you know. Not even good friends."

"Right."

It was all kind of new.

-CHAPTER TWELVE-
THE RIDE

"Were your parents mad?" Oliver asked.

Ella slumped on the curb and picked at her ratty jeans. They were waiting for her mom to give them a ride to the historical society after school.

"Yeah," she said. "I got one of those long lectures with lots of hand motions."

"I hate those."

"Once you learn how to tune it out, it's not so bad." Ella checked her phone again. "Thanks, by the way."

"Sure." Oliver knew what she meant. *Thanks for covering up my lie about not texting my mom.* The question, obviously, was *why* Ella hadn't texted her mom in the first place, but Oliver wasn't sure their social-studies-partner-just-barely-friendship entitled him to ask personal questions.

"Remember when I came over to your house, and you warned me about your mom?" Ella asked.

"Yeah."

"I need to warn you about mine: She'll probably be on her phone most of the time. And if she's not, she'll be asking you stupid questions about things that don't matter or telling you things about our family that don't matter. You can just ignore her if you don't want to answer. It's what I do."

"Thanks for the heads-up."

Ella checked her phone again. "She probably got stuck at some house showing."

"I don't really have anything else to do."

Ella looked up at a car headed their way. "Predictable."

A black Mercedes pulled up to the curb. "Hey baby," a man called out the window. "Mom's at a showing. I'm giving you a ride."

"Told you," Ella muttered as she slid into the car.

Oliver followed.

Ella's dad's phone rang.

"Give me the good news," he said.

"Financing came through." The faraway voice came through the speakers and made the whole car thump.

"How's the rate?"

"Best you're gonna get in this economy. You'd almost think those Weller boys don't want to make money."

"I'm not complaining." Mr. Berry drum-rolled on the steering wheel. "Email me the terms, I'll review them when I get back to the office."

"Done."

Mr. Berry hit a button on the steering wheel to hang up. "Sorry, guys. I've been waiting for that news all day."

Ella stared out the window. Of course. Oliver caught Mr. Berry's eye in the rearview mirror and wasn't sure what to do. He waved.

"Hi. I'm Oliver."

"Hey, Oliver. I'm Jonathan."

"I'm not allowed to call adults by their first names. My mom's pretty firm on that."

"Okay."

"I can call you Mr. B if you want, but that's about as far as I can go."

". . . Mr. B it is."

The streets clogged up the minute they turned off the main road. Construction. Oliver noticed the familiar diamond Weller logo on the corner.

"Great spot for a gas station, huh?" Mr. Berry said.

Ella snorted like she was trying to clear out some mucus.

"My mom always says they should put one there," Oliver said. "She said there would be one there if it wasn't for all the yuppies. I don't really know who they are but apparently there's a lot of them here."

"People in town don't want things getting more crowded," Mr. Berry said. "That's why they block building projects like that. Took me almost five years to buy that lot."

"You own that land?"

"Yup."

Oliver looked at Ella, who looked ready to jump out the window. "What are you gonna do with it?"

"My company leased it to another company who's building a gas station there. Tell your mom the yuppies lost a round."

"Wow." So it was official—Ella's parents were loaded.

"But you should really thank *them*," Mr. Berry continued, pointing to the Weller sign as they passed it. "They fund almost all my deals."

Oliver looked to Ella for some help carrying this conversation. Nothing. He looked at the brick storefronts out his window. Boring. He looked ahead at the traffic. Tons.

And Ella's dad was still talking. "You can borrow money for just about anything. The deals I've made with their financing are putting Ella's sister through college—and you too, baby," he called back.

The car stopped again. Oliver could see the courthouse, three traffic lights ahead. The historical society was right around here.

Ella opened the door and dragged her backpack out behind her.

"Ella, we're not—" her dad started.

"We'll walk," she shouted back.

CHAPTER THIRTEEN

THE HISTORICAL SOCIETY
OF BOREDOM

Oliver did one of those awkward run-skip-walks to catch up with her.

". . . never shuts up about it," Ella mumbled.

"What?"

She glared back toward the Mercedes like she wanted to commit murder.

"Hang on." Oliver could barely keep up with her. "I think we just passed it."

Ella finally slowed down. "Sorry I didn't warn you about him—I didn't know he was coming."

"It's okay." Oliver got out his phone. He checked out the nearest street sign, and pointed across the road to a building. "It's that one."

They jaywalked to the other side and looked up at the small stone house with black shutters. Slate steps led up to a porch supported by two white columns, with a black door that had a bronze plaque in the center. DOYLESTOWN HISTORICAL SOCIETY, it read. Oliver wasn't that cool, but even he knew that this was the kind of place where Civil War coolness went to die.

Ella charged up the steps and opened the door.

Oliver followed her into a cramped living room that somebody had turned into an office lobby. There were big rugs over wooden floors, a fireplace, a few side tables, and like twenty chairs from an ancient century. In one of those chairs slept a man old enough to be from one of those centuries. Or maybe he'd just died of boredom.

"Should I poke him?" Ella whispered.

Oliver spotted a fire iron along the wall. No. That would be really awkward if he was sleeping or dead.

He shook his head.

"Then what?"

Oliver looked around, and then shoved the door closed so it made a loud *bang*.

"No grapes," the old man mumbled. Then he went back to sleep.

"At least we know he's alive," Oliver whispered.

Ella motioned to a side table next to Oliver that had a giant book near the edge. "Push it off."

"I don't know why we're still whispering," he said in a normal voice.

Ella clamped her hand over her mouth as she snorted. Oliver shoved the book to the floor.

Thud.

"Myrtle Beach!" the old man shouted. He shot straight up to a standing position, put his hands in his pockets, and swayed like an elm tree in the wind. "Hello there."

"Uh, hi," Oliver said. "I'm Oliver. This is Ella. We're from Kennesaw Middle School . . . Mr. Carrow's class . . . we're researching—"

"Raymond Stone." The man's eyes lit up like Private Stone was some sort of super soldier who singlehandedly won the war with his bayonet. "Mr. Carrow said you'd be over. This way." He waved for them to follow down the hall. "I'm Mr. Daniels, the weekday caretaker of this place. We don't get many visitors, so sometimes I doze off. Don't tell my boss."

"Uh, okay." Oliver wondered how they got any visitors, ever. He completely got the dozing-off part.

The old man chuckled. "Just joking. I'm the boss. Guess you could say I'd have to fire myself."

"Right."

"This is the main research area," Mr. Daniels said, leading them into the next room. It was a little bigger than the entryway and had two reading tables in the center. Bookshelves lined one wall and some computer stations took up the other. There was a guy typing on one of them who looked like he played computer games for a living. Oliver wasn't really sure how old he was. High school, maybe? College? It was hard to tell with computer game people. Oliver waved. The guy dumped some M&M's in his mouth.

"That's Hal, one of our volunteers," Mr. Daniels said. "He does a lot of transcription work for us—taking primary sources and digitizing them. He's the one who put together Stone's little biography for the website using county and military records. But I think the story you're looking for is in here." He pulled a big white file box off a shelf and gently put it down in front of them like it was full of gold.

Ella took the lid off. "Awesome."

Oliver rolled his eyes.

"Not a fan of primary sources?" Mr. Daniels asked.

"More a fan of battles."

"Give it a chance." His eyes did that sparkly thing again. "You never know what interesting things you might discover in uninteresting places."

Like discovering that I have a fatal allergy to study-ing soldiers who died of diarrhea, Oliver thought.

Mr. Daniels pulled a three-ring binder out of the box. "You're the first to get a peek, so I'd be grateful if you could inventory the items as you go. And you'll notice they're all in protective sleeves; if you take them out the oils of your skin will speed up the decay." He pointed to a box of latex gloves next to Hal. "Put on a pair of those if you really have to handle something."

Hal put a hand on top of the latex glove box without looking away from the computer screen.

"If you have any questions, you should ask him. Hal knows more about navigating documents than most historians."

"Is there a bathroom?" Oliver asked.

Mr. Daniels rapped on a door in the hall as he passed it. Oliver took a step toward it, but something grabbed his shirt.

"If you think you're leaving me with *him,* you're insane," she whispered, eyeing Hal.

"But I have to pee."

Hal's chair squeaked as it spun slowly around. He ate some M&M's, and then completed the revolution back to the screen.

"Okay," Oliver said. "I'll just hold it."

They pulled chairs to the farthest possible spot from Hal and unpacked their stuff. By the time Oliver had his notes out, Ella was already squinting at the first letter.

"The writing is so tiny," she said.

Oliver leaned closer, but it all just looked like swirly lines. "Is that English?"

"It's cursive. We learned it in fifth grade."

"Yeah—our names."

Ella inspected the letter through its protective sheet. "Philadelphia, October second, 1862."

"How can you read that?"

"I went to private school until third grade. We were only allowed to write in cursive. Haven't done it in a while, but it'll come back." She gave her laptop to him. "You type it up as I read it."

Sixty-seven minutes later—Oliver knew because he counted every one—they'd transcribed eight letters.

"This is incredibly boring," he said. "And now I *really* have to pee."

"I think it's pretty interesting."

"Interesting?" Oliver scrolled up. *"Dear Mother: I received your letter from the 12th and 21st this morning. Home. How much pleasure there is in that word. The last eight days have been trying ones for the regiment. We have been kept constantly moving, and were almost starved. Many of the regiment have the flux, including me. Tell Father I do not regret my service even though he does."*

He went to the next one.

"Dear Sister: Here I am at last in Dixie on a rise of ground one mile and a half from the Capital. How long we are going to stay I don't know. A man came along with a load of apples and offered them to us. I thought of Father taking the corn to Philadelphia without me and hope he is getting on with the hired hand. A word or two I should like from him." Oliver made a snoring sound. "You think that's interesting?"

"Yeah."

"But there's no fighting. Zero. He's just talking about people he bumped into from his hometown, food, walking, and his geographic location."

"War isn't just about fighting."

"Uh, I'm pretty sure it's mostly about fighting."

"I guess, but fighting only took up a small percentage of a soldier's life. I think that's what Mr. Carrow is trying to make us see: that fighting is just part of the story."

"Maybe fighting took up less time, but it's definitely the most important part. It's what I've been practicing for."

"Oh, right—your reenactment club."

"It's not a club—it's a regiment."

"Regiment, right."

"We've been drilling for almost a year to get ready for the big three-day Gettysburg reenactment in July.

I mean, it's big every year, but this year it's *really* big because it's during the actual one-hundred-and-fiftieth anniversary."

Ella looked straight at him. "When's your next session?"

"It's called—"

"Yeah, drill. When's the next one?"

"Uh, why?"

"I want to see it."

"Why?"

"I could record some footage for the documentary. I think it's called B-roll—like for showing without sound during a narration," Ella said. "Plus it sounds pretty cool."

"Oh." Something warm spread from the center of Oliver's chest up to his face. He had the strange urge to get up and high-five Ella, even though he wasn't the type of person who got or gave high fives.

"What?"

"Uh, nothing. It's just no one's ever said that about it before. That it's cool."

"That's because people are usually too busy doing stuff other people tell them is cool to see what is actually cool," Ella said. "Like all those publishers who read *Harry Potter* but rejected it because they were too busy reading other books they thought would sell better."

"Yeah," Oliver said. "Or like those people at the China Buffet who start with the salad bar."

"*Exactly.* Or like when your mom hears some stupid singer all over the radio and thinks she's the world's best mom for buying you concert tickets, even though if she'd stop working for one second and listen, she'd know you hate all that radio crap."

Oliver blinked. He'd missed something.

"Right," he said. "Drill is on Saturdays from ten to noon."

"Tomorrow?" Ella frowned. "I can't go. I'm grounded 'cause of the texting thing."

"Oh, right." Shoot. Suddenly he really wanted her there. She thought it was cool. "Maybe next week."

"Yeah, I guess."

"You'd probably sweat to death, anyway," Oliver said, trying to make her feel better. "My mom doesn't even stay when it's this hot. She tells my dad she's jogging but she really goes to Home Goods and looks for sales."

Ella shrugged it off and flipped to the next letter.

"*July 6, 1863. Gettysburg, Pennsylvania. Dear Mrs. Stone . . . As you in all probability have not heard of the death of your son, and as I was witness to his death, I consider it my duty to write you. Raymond passed in the night, having suffered of flux for many months.*

He was very brave in the face of death and thanked our Lord Jesus Christ that he could give his life for his country. He spoke often of his father, wanting him to know that he did not regret enlisting even though he never saw the battlefield. He said the farm would be taken care of in his death, and prayed that you would not worry. With this letter are his things. I am sorry for your loss. Sincerely, Susanna Wentworth."

Oliver finished typing and saved the document. "My mom said she wanted us to wait outside anyway. If we don't, she'll definitely use the horn and it'll be really embarrassing."

"Ollie—we basically just read his last words. Have some respect."

He watched her examine the letter in silence. "It's not like he was Captain America or something."

"What does that mean?"

"I just mean it's not like he died making some heroic charge at Gettysburg. He died of diarrhea, off the battlefield. He never even fought."

Ella stared at him for a second. "Just because he didn't die in an epic battle doesn't mean his story isn't important."

"I didn't say he wasn't important."

"Just not important enough to do a project on."

Oliver examined her face, and it told him that answering honestly was not a good idea.

Beeeep-beeeeeeeeeeeep went the van's horn.

"She knows it's embarrassing," Oliver said. "That's why she does it."

Ella looked at the letter a little longer before slowly putting the binder back in the cardboard box. As they walked out of the research room, Oliver half waved to Hal, which reminded him—he had a question.

"Uh, Hal."

Hal rotated around slowly. "Yes?"

His voice was a little whinier than Oliver had imagined for such a big guy.

"You're sure Stone joined the 68th down in Philly and not the 104th?" Oliver asked.

Hal clicked around a little and curled his index finger for Oliver to come closer. Oliver shuffled over and peered at a scanned-in parchment ledger with—get this—more cursive writing. "This is a muster roll for the 68th Pennsylvania Volunteers," Hal said.

It was bookmarked, which Oliver found to be awesome. He followed Hal's chubby finger halfway down a column labeled NAME until he found it. Raymond Stone. Farther to the right under DATE it said *Sept. 3, 1862.*

Beeeep-beeeeep-beeeeeeeeeeeeeeeep.

"Okay," Oliver said. "Thanks."

He turned back at the hallway.

"I don't get it: Why would a soldier from here enlist with a regiment in Philadelphia?"

Hal shrugged.

And opened another packet of M&M's.

-CHAPTER FOURTEEN-
THE PROBLEM WITH WOOL TROUSERS

It was hot and humid and so freaking sunny at the park that Oliver wondered if the earth had slipped its orbit and drifted closer to the late-May sun. His wool pants felt like ten layers of sheepskin. He was literally drenched in sweat.

"Attention company!" shouted the large, bearded Sergeant Tom. The sound echoed across the public park's open field and reached a few mid-morning runners suffering under the beating rays.

Oliver locked his knees, threw his shoulders back, and held his left arm rigid against the seam of his wool trousers. His right hand was busy keeping the rifle from slipping onto the ground—the most embarrassing thing you could ever do as a Civil War reenactor.

"In each rank, count—oh crap."

A body hit the ground somewhere to Oliver's right. He wasn't about to break rank—this was war, people. Sliding his eyes as far as he could without moving his head, Oliver saw the ripped wool trouser seat of a giant rear end. It was hard to tell who it was, as a lot of the 104th Pennsylvania Volunteers could generally be categorized as large.

"Give me your canteen, Joe," Sergeant Tom said to the closest soldier.

"Sorry, Tom—drank it all," panted Joe.

"Permission to break rank, Sergeant," Oliver shouted.

"What? Yeah, of course, Oliver. Granted."

Oliver sprinted to Sergeant Tom and gave him his canteen.

"Thanks, Ollie. Joe, help me roll him over."

"I think I'm gonna faint myself," Joe said, kneeling down. He was the only soldier in the 104th without a beard (aside from Oliver) because he managed a bank and wasn't allowed to look like a Civil War reenactor prepping hardcore for the 150th anniversary of the Battle of Gettysburg. The lack of beard let Oliver see water dripping off the fleshy, jiggly part under Joe's chin.

"I'll help," Oliver said as the rest of the regiment— all nine of them who had decided to come out on this blazing hot morning—looked on in concern.

"On three," Sergeant Tom said. They heaved the soldier over and dumped some water on his face. "Frank, you okay?"

"Should I call 911?" Joe asked.

"No, he's fine," Sergeant Tom said. "Just fainted. And gave himself a bloody nose."

Frank patted his face and stared at the blood in confusion. "What happened?"

"You got shot," Joe said. "Don't worry, I'll take good care of your truck."

"You fainted," Sergeant Tom grunted, helping Frank sit up. "Let's get you to the pavilion."

It took the two men ten minutes to get Frank to the pavilion. Oliver carried the fallen soldier's weapon.

"I think that's good for today," Sergeant Tom said to the remaining members of the 104th who hadn't already gone to their cars and driven the heck home. "See everybody next week. Check your email in case I have to change the drill field; I think I saw a flyer about Ultimate Frisbee or something happening here next weekend."

"Glad my crew wasn't here to see this," Frank said, holding a dirty cloth from Sergeant Tom's knapsack to his nose.

"I said in the email it was going to be hot, and to drink lots of water."

"Coffee has water in it."

"Coffee is a diuretic. It dehydrates you."

He handed Frank a bottle of water from the pavilion cooler and Frank downed it. "Thanks for not leaving me on the field of battle. Johnny Reb would have made off with my shoes, rifle, and the rest of my coffee."

"You should thank Ollie," Sergeant Tom said. "It was his canteen that brought you back to the land of the living."

Frank gave a tired salute. "Private Prichard: I hereby award you a Medal of Honor for keeping me alive long enough to see my daughter graduate high school."

"No problem."

Frank shifted on the bench and winced. "Feels like I got a splinter in my butt."

"Your pants ripped when you fell," Joe said.

Oliver was glad to be out of the heat, but kind of sad drill had been cut short by an hour. To be completely honest, he was also kind of uncomfortable. For all the Saturday mornings he'd spent with these grown men, he didn't really know them well enough to be relaxed sitting around waiting for his mom.

"I have a question about the regiment," Oliver said. If he was going to have an awkward morning, he might as well get some use out of the situation. "Did you have to live around here to enlist in the 104th? Or was it open to anybody?"

"Mostly regiments were made up of men from the local area," Sergeant Tom said. "But they'd take someone from another town, if that's what you mean."

"So a kid from around here could go down to the city and enlist there?"

"Sure, yeah."

"Huh." Oliver picked at the plastic ring on his bottle. "Why would somebody do that?"

Sergeant Tom shrugged. "Maybe they weren't sure if they wanted to fight when the local regiment was mustered into service. Could've changed their mind and then joined up with another regiment when they mustered."

"Right. That makes sense."

"Why the interest?" asked Frank.

"Just something for this school project," Oliver said. He knew it shouldn't really matter, but for some reason it did—like he was up on his mountain of facts, and found a rock that had no business being there, but was. He had to make sense of it.

"Hi."

Oliver turned his head.

Ella Berry.

Standing at the other end of the pavilion.

CHAPTER FIFTEEN

B-ROLL

Despite the ridiculous humidity, Ella's hair looked less messy. She also wore jean shorts and a tank top that wasn't exactly dirty. It actually fit, too.

"Uh, hey," he said. "What's up?"

"I'm here to watch you drill."

That warm feeling was back in his chest. Or maybe it was the slaughtering humidity. "I thought you were grounded."

"I told my mom it was for school and she caved." Ella looked around. "Where's everyone else?"

"That's a good question, young lady," Sergeant Tom said.

"They retreated to air-conditioning like sensible soldiers," Frank said between swigs.

"Everyone," Oliver said, "this is Ella."

"A gentleman never sits when a lady is present,"

Sergeant Tom said, nudging Oliver to stand. "Walking wounded excluded, of course," he added with a nod at Frank.

He offered her a water and she took a giant Ella gulp.

"So how do you two know each other?" Sergeant Tom asked.

"We're doing a social studies project together," Oliver said.

"It's about this Union private named Raymond Stone who was from around here," Ella said. "We're making a documentary about his war experience based on the letters he wrote home. I was hoping to get some B-roll footage of you guys drilling."

"We had to stop early because of the heat," Oliver said.

"Just like the actual Battle of Gettysburg," Ella said. "Did you know that on the third day it got up to eighty-seven degrees? Lots of soldiers fainted from heat exhaustion."

Oliver smiled. She'd been reading up on the battle. Cool.

"We'll be here again next week," Sergeant Tom said. "You're welcome to come back."

She looked at her phone and then at Oliver. "My mom won't be back for a little. I could get some footage now of just you doing some stuff. We could overlay the letters on the footage as you read them out loud, like in those Ken Burns movies."

"You've been watching Ken Burns?" Oliver asked.

"A little."

He grinned. Very cool. "Yeah. Okay. How about over there, in the shade under those trees."

"Ever thought about reenacting?" Sergeant Tom asked. "We could use a nurse with your passion. Last one in this regiment was Frank's daughter, but she spent the whole time texting."

Ella drained the rest of her water and threw the bottle in the giant trash barrel. Swish. "If I ever reenacted, I think I'd be one of those girls who dressed up as a guy to enlist—you know?"

Frank let out a booming laugh. Oliver grabbed the older rifle Sergeant Tom let him borrow for drill and led the way.

"They're nice," Ella said.

"Yeah."

"Did that guy really faint?"

"Yeah. He's pretty tough, though. He runs a construction company."

"It's really interesting," she said. "All these people with regular lives who secretly love the Civil War. I never thought about it before. They're like secret magicians: No one knows what they know or what they can do."

"Like you and your card trick," Oliver said.

"Yeah, I guess so." She looked around the grove. "Sit against this tree, like you're in camp writing a letter. I brought some stuff."

"Okay."

She pulled an inkwell pen from her backpack—black with an ornate gold tip. "Took this from my dad's office. It was a gift from his business partner or something."

"Won't he be upset?"

"Who cares?" Clearly she didn't. "And I made this last night. What do you think?"

She held up a piece of legit parchment paper. "You *made* this?" Oliver asked.

"I stained it with tea and then crumpled it up. Used up pretty much all the teabags we had."

"It looks exactly like the paper Stone wrote on." The letters were lame, but this was pretty cool. Oliver set his rifle against the tree and took off his cap.

"What's that little triangle on your shirt mean?" she asked.

"Unit ID." Oliver ran his finger over the white badge his mom had sewn on. It was one of the coolest parts of his uniform. "The triangle means I'm part of the Union

Army's Fourth Corps, and the white means the Second Division. General Hooker made it standard when he got command of the army in 1863. It's one of the few not-embarrassing things he did while in charge."

"Cool." Ella took out a small tripod from her backpack and snapped her iPhone to some contraption on the top. "Okay. Let's do a couple from the front. Just act normal; pretend you're writing home."

Oliver obeyed.

Ella flipped the tripod around and showed him the footage when she was done. "You like it?"

"I look kinda wimpy, to be honest."

"Really? I think you look like a lot of soldiers probably did. Young and sweaty."

Better than wimpy. "Thanks."

"Plus it will look better once we put an older filter over the footage." She set the camera behind him. "Okay. Same thing again."

They filmed a bunch more writing shots from different positions and got some cool ones of Oliver marching and fake firing the rifle. Eventually Ella's iPhone ran out of space, which was fine because her mom's giant white Escalade pulled into the parking lot five minutes later.

"You need a ride home?" Ella asked as she packed up.

"Uh, no—it's okay. My mom is probably almost here."

"*Almost* can be a long time in my experience. Why don't you call her to make sure."

Oliver's mom picked up on the second ring. "Ollie—everything okay?"

"Yeah, fine. Um, drill ended early because of the heat. How close are you?"

"Give me about twenty minutes. The checkout line looks really long."

"Uh, well, Ella's mom is here; Ella came to get some footage for the documentary. I'll get a ride with her."

"Oh—great. Perfect."

He hung up. "Still okay if I go with you?"

"Yup."

They were halfway to the Escalade when Ella started in about her mom.

"Don't forget what I said about her—the phone and stupid stuff she'll talk about."

"Right." What Oliver was really wondering was how Ella's mom felt about wool trouser butt sweat on her leather seats, because there was for sure going to be some of that happening up in this Escalade. "Thanks for the ride home."

"Friends don't let friends sit around in wool pants sweating to death waiting for their moms," Ella said. She put her fist out toward him. "Pound it."

Oliver stared at her outstretched fist. "What?"

"Make a fist." Ella knocked her knuckles against his. "That's called pounding it."

"I've seen people do that. I always thought it would hurt."

"Now you know it doesn't."

-CHAPTER SIXTEEN-
THE MOM

"That's the offer, Carla," said Ella's mom. Her voice stabbed the air in sharp thrusts like a bayonet. "My client is ready to move forward on two other homes and that's not a threat. It's the truth."

She smiled and waved to Ella and Oliver through the rearview mirror—one of those finger-flexing waves with a lot of energy behind it. She did not stop talking.

"You're not listening to me—my client won't budge. They know exactly what you and I know: that they could get another thousand square feet in Solebury for ten percent less than this offer."

She mouthed "I'm sorry" into the mirror.

"She's not," Ella said toward her window. Or at least that's what Oliver thought she said. The Escalade was giant; Ella was like ten feet away.

"Well, that's up to you. . . . All right. I'll tell them, but don't be surprised if the next time you call me I'm at escrow. . . . Uh-huh. Bu-bye." She pushed a button on her earpiece and fluffed her lion mane of golden hair. "Sorry about that. I've been trying to close this deal for a week."

"Uh, it's okay," Oliver said. He thought he should say *something,* since the lady was giving him a ride home. Like usual, Ella clearly had no plans to participate in the conversation.

"The weekend is my busiest time," Ella's mom said as she turned the white leather wheel with one hand. Oliver saw her glance at the phone in her other hand, and wondered if she knew you're not supposed to text and drive. "Did Ella tell you I sell houses?"

Ella snorted.

"Yeah," Oliver said.

"It's my life." Mrs. Berry sighed. "Lots of weekend hours, but I do love it."

"My mom works at Home Depot. She helps people pick out the right type of paint for whatever their project is. And she operates the machine that puts in the color dye and shakes it around."

"That's . . . interesting," Mrs. Berry said. "I'll have to say hello to her the next time I'm there. I've been wanting to redo our great room ever since Ella's father brought in that ridiculous fourteen-foot Christmas tree last year. I told him it would scrape the walls and of course, I was right."

Ella stared at Oliver deadpan: *See?*

"My dad sells meat." Oliver really needed to find better transitions between his stream of consciousness and the ongoing conversation.

"Ah-ha. I see. At the grocery store?"

"No, like between slaughterhouses and suppliers. My G-Pop owned a meat processing plant and my dad and uncles grew up working there. Then the plant shut down and my dad went into the meat-selling business. He basically sells cuts of meat like a stock trader sells stocks. I don't really understand it all, but that's the analogy he gives."

"I see." Mrs. Berry adjusted the rearview mirror. "Charlie would find that interesting—Ella's older sister. She just finished her second year at Wharton and is thinking about corporate finance."

Oliver heard a slight *bang* as Ella rested her head against the window. It was like the entire conversation was pushing her further away.

"Ella can make a card disappear into thin air." For some reason declaring that made him feel better—like he was pulling her back.

"Ella can . . . I'm sorry—what?"

"She can make a card vanish and then bring it back again." Oliver saw Ella's reflection smiling a little in the window, and he knew he'd been right to say something.

"If this was colonial times, they'd probably think she was a witch and burn her alive. It's that good."

"Ah . . . I'll have to see that. Ella, sweetie, I didn't know you did card tricks."

Silence.

Mrs. Berry smiled really widely and turned up the radio.

Oliver's phone buzzed and he slid it out of his wool trousers.

A text from Ella: *Thanks.*

Pound it.

LOL. You don't usually text it. You just do it.

OK.

Oliver reached over the aisle with his fist.

Ella pounded it.

What's Wharton? he asked.

Who cares?

They exchanged crooked smiles.

When I get out, don't look at the seat, Oliver typed.

???

I think I'm sweating through the leather.

Haha. You ARE wearing wool pants.

Trousers.

You ARE wearing wool trousers.

Ella's mom turned into Oliver's driveway and pulled up behind the crappy family van.

"Thanks again for the ride," he said.

"You're welcome, Oliver."

"See ya," Ella said.

Oliver opened the door and slid out. He couldn't stand to look back at the leather seat to check for the butt sweat that was definitely there.

At the front door his phone buzzed again.

Ella: *No trouser sweat.*

Really?

:)

CHAPTER SEVENTEEN

SOME GUY

"I thought she wasn't supposed to play on Sundays," Oliver said at breakfast the next morning. Addie had been at it since seven, stopping only to shovel down pancakes before racing back. "You said God rested on Sundays and so should our eardrums."

Oliver's dad washed a skillet while his mom drank coffee and flipped through a cooking magazine.

"When did I say that?" his dad asked.

"On the way home from her last recital."

"I thought you were asleep," Oliver's mom said.

"I wasn't."

"Then you were eavesdropping."

"It's only eavesdropping if I was listening in secret." Oliver forked in a last bite of his dad's Sunday pancakes and washed it down with OJ. "I was just listening."

"Then listen up," his mom said. "I'll have Addie run some errands with your dad if you weed the front bed."

Oliver rinsed his plate and put it in the dishwasher. "I'll just put my headphones on."

In the basement Oliver dove back into the Time-Life Civil War hardback he'd been reading on the Battle of Gettysburg. The headphones drowned out enough of Addie's banging that he could focus on the super-detailed battle map with a billion captions. This was where the gold was—not the boring letters of Private Nobody.

Oliver stared at the 104th Regimental flag hanging on the wall—the regiment Stone should have enlisted with. The detail itched worse. He thought about Stone's letters, and about Mr. Daniels saying that interesting things are sometimes found in horribly boring places.

And then he grabbed his book bag and raced up the steps to flag down his dad as he pulled out of the driveway.

"Sure it's open on a Sunday?" Oliver's dad asked as they slowed at the historical society.

"The guy who runs it said he hangs out here on the weekends."

"I'm not sure about leaving you here by yourself."

"He's not a creeper, Dad. He's just old." Oliver got out of the van and tried the knob on the historical society's front door. It was open. "See you an in hour," he called.

Oliver walked inside and saw Mr. Daniels, asleep in his chair. Instead of waking him, he went to the research room and set up shop at one of the computer stations. It was kind of nice to have the place to himself. It was nice not to have Hal there, being super weird. Or Ella, being super excited. He could finally get something real done, working alone.

Oliver opened a Word doc and got started.

Why did Stone join the 68th?

Theory #1: Stone didn't know if he wanted to fight or not when the 104th mustered into service. Later he decided to fight, and found a regiment that was forming—the 68th in Philly.

Theory #2: Stone was so ready to fight that he couldn't wait for his local town to form a regiment. He went to Philly and joined the 68th.

How to prove:

- Look up the muster dates of both regiments to see which one was first
- Find a letter where Stone talks about it.

Oliver's logic was pretty simple: The regiment that mustered into service first, plus the amount of time between each regiment's muster date, would tell the story.

Oliver combed through ten pages of Google results before he found a Penn State University database that had digitized all the individual regimental history. He felt himself slipping into a trance of awesomeness as he scrolled through the index.

Oliver found the 68th's regimental history first. It was a digitized book, so he had to wait a few seconds for the page to appear every time he clicked forward.

"September 3, 1862," he said. "Bingo."

Bookmarking the page, Oliver backtracked to the index and found the 104th's history—the local regiment Stone should have enlisted with.

"Huh," Oliver said.

August 25, 1862.

"So you chose not to enlist with your local regiment," Oliver said to the empty research room. "Instead, you went down to Philly a week later and enlisted with a bunch of strangers. That doesn't make any sense."

"Who are you talking to?"

Mr. Daniels stood in the doorway, scratching his head of white hair.

"Uh, nobody," Oliver said. "Just thinking out loud."

"I used to do that too until my wife tried to have me committed."

"Uh-huh."

Mr. Daniels scanned Oliver's Word doc. "This looks interesting."

"Uh, I guess. I'm kinda stuck, actually."

"My brother was a detective. He used to say the key to solving a case was talking about it over and over. Let's hear it."

Oliver summarized what he had so far.

"So the dates don't really tell me anything," he finished. "I still don't know why Stone would join the 68th—a regiment almost sixty miles from his house, full of total strangers, when his own town formed one a week earlier."

"I think the dates are helpful," Mr. Daniels said. "They eliminate your first two theories. Now you can move on to a third."

"I don't have a third."

"No, you don't." Mr. Daniels headed back to the study with a wave. "Not yet."

And Oliver was alone with his big question again.

Why did Stone join the 68th?

Theory #1: ~~Stone didn't know if he wanted to fight or not when the 104th mustered into service. Later he decided to fight, and found a regiment that was forming—the 68th in Philly.~~

Theory #2: ~~Stone was so ready to fight that~~

~~he couldn't wait for his local town to form a~~
~~regiment. He went to Philly and joined the 68th.~~
How to prove:
- ~~Look up the muster dates of both regiments~~
~~to see which one was first~~
- Find a letter where Stone talks about it.

Oliver eyed the shelf across the room with all the Private Stone letters.

"Fine," he said. "Fine."

Without Ella, it was pretty much impossible to read Stone's handwriting. Oliver almost ran out of binder pages looking for one he could actually transcribe.

Philadelphia, Pennsylvania
December 20, 1862

Mr. Stone,
The papers inform me that Raymond's regiment is
stationed outside the Capital. I pray he is safe and
in good health. May this great nation be reunited
and your son returned to you safely. But if our Lord
should see fit to take him, may you find comfort that
He shall witness the fulfillment of the agreement
contracted between us.

Your humble servant,
H. Weller

Oliver stared at the author's name. *H. Weller.* Why was that name so familiar?

Another line pricked Oliver's mind.

But if our Lord should see fit to take him, may you find comfort that He shall witness the fulfillment of the agreement contracted between us.

"Him," Oliver said. "As in you." At this point, he was weirdly okay with talking out loud to a very dead Private Raymond Stone. "So if you die, this guy is going to fulfill some contract he made with your dad. Or you. The 'us' is kind of just hanging there."

Oliver felt like he'd just found a secret cave high up his Civil War mountain, except the cave was only ten feet deep and totally empty.

"That doesn't make any sense. At all."

"Interesting things," shouted Mr. Daniels from the foyer. "In the most uninteresting places."

Oliver's phone went off; his dad was out front. Time flew when you were on the mountain. Oliver put all the documents back and stared at his notes. Most of the page had lines through it.

Before closing the Word doc, he added one more bullet point:

• What did Stone agree to????

CHAPTER EIGHTEEN

THE HEAD WRITING CONSULTANT

"I like it," Oliver said.

Ella sunk her teeth into cafeteria pizza as she watched the footage on her giant iPhone screen. The orange sauce matched a stain on her shirt, but not from today. Back to the messy weekday outfits. "It's missing something."

Oliver tapped the screen to replay the opening minute of their documentary-under-construction. The black screen faded to blue as their working title appeared: *The Wartime Experience of Private Raymond Stone* by Ella Berry and Oliver Prichard. Footage of Oliver marching in the park cross-dissolved with him thrusting the bayonet; then he was sitting down against the tree writing; then some shots of his face covered in sweat. Over everything, Oliver's voice narrated a few lines from one of Stone's early (and epically boring) letters.

Then the screen went black.

Oliver chewed on his ham sandwich. "It's fine."

"It's missing something," Ella repeated.

"It's missing a storyline," said Kevin, who had peeked over during the first viewing before going back to his typing. "And a little heavy on the cross-dissolve, if we're getting picky."

"What do you mean—storyline?" Ella asked.

"You just jump right in with random footage. Does this guy have a home or what? Was he born on the battlefield? What about his past? Does he have a family? A wife? Why is he fighting?"

"It's supposed to be about his wartime experience," Oliver said.

"But you need some human interest stuff if you want the audience to care." Kevin turned over a napkin and drew a really crappy triangle. "This is a story plot: starts here at the bottom with the background—where he grew up, family, all that. Then it starts going up. That's called the rising action—the war breaking out, his decision to enlist, blah blah blah." Kevin's pen reached the peak of the triangle. "This is the climax— the highpoint of the story. Like a battle where he proved his valor or something. Then it goes down to the falling action—he goes home—and ends here at the bottom: the resolution. He marries his one true love. They have ten babies. Whatever."

"Our soldier died after the Battle of Gettysburg," Ella said.

Kevin raised one eyebrow really high. "A tragedy . . . hmmm . . ."

"A what?" Oliver asked.

"Your hero dies at the end, which makes it a tragedy."

"He died of diarrhea," Oliver said, just to clarify the situation in case that changed Kevin's definition of "hero."

"A little messy—pun intended, you're welcome—but still a tragedy. The kind of story that lives with the reader forever—not like comedies."

"It's not supposed to be funny."

"He means it focuses on death instead of life," Ella said. "Mrs. Mason said all stories are one or the other."

"When did she say that?" Oliver said.

"In book club."

"You're in Mrs. Mason's book club?"

"Yeah."

Kevin snapped a finger and pointed at her. "That's where I know you from."

"But you have a D in English," Oliver said. "Why would you go to book club?"

"I like to read."

"So you like to read for fun—which means you obviously can read—but you're almost failing English. Which means you're definitely almost failing on purpose, right?"

Ella moved the playhead on her phone screen back and forth, frowning. "Yeah."

"Why?"

She snorted. "Did you forget both car rides with my parents?"

"You're tanking English because of your parents."

Firm nod.

"To piss them off?"

"You're getting warmer."

Oliver wanted to ask if the reason covered Ella's general appearance too, but thought that might be pushing it.

Ella bit a nail as she rewatched the opening scene. "Kevin's right. We need a storyline."

"Okay."

Oliver looked at Kevin. Kevin stared back.

Then it hit Oliver.

"Kevin. You should help us. This is kind of your thing."

"Hmmm." Kevin clicked his tongue. "What's the pay?"

"Uh, nothing."

"You drive a hard bargain."

Oliver took a second to think. "What if I could get you that A in English?"

"Explain."

"Mrs. Mason won't give you extra credit for the Wattpad stories because they don't line up with state standards or whatever. But our project probably does."

"That's brilliant," Ella said. "But we'll have to get Mr. Carrow on board too. Kevin—what do you think?"

He tilted his head side to side. "If it works, I can spend Resource doing some actual writing instead of wishing for a global disaster."

"That's true," Oliver said.

"Big question: What's the snack situation at your house?"

"My mom buys Cheez-Its by the barrel."

"How about drinks?"

"Capri Suns."

"Variety pack?"

"I'll see what I can do."

"Deal." Kevin thrust out his hand and shook both of theirs. "Consider me on board as Head Writing Consultant."

"You're the only writing consultant," Oliver said.

"And let's keep it that way."

Ella stuffed about ten French fries into her mouth and didn't bother to swallow before she said, "Now. We need a plan."

CHAPTER NINETEEN

THE DEAL

"Good to go on my end," Oliver whispered to Kevin and Ella as he joined them in Mrs. Mason's room after school. "I had Carrow look up Kevin's grades like we talked about and he was pretty impressed."

"Mason didn't say much when Kevin explained it. Just a lot of staring," Ella said. "She was still mad that he was on his phone during Resource."

"It felt like she was staring into my soul," Kevin said. "And my soul didn't meet her standards."

Mr. Carrow came in and closed the door. "How about this, Mrs. Mason—students asking to do *more* work. It's like they're on a mission to learn or something. I think we should get a raise."

"They do seem . . . eager," Mrs. Mason said.

"Okay gang, here's the deal: Mrs. Mason and I are

on board with this. Actually, we think your little col-laboration is pretty cool."

"But there are guidelines," Mrs. Mason said. "First, and most important: You take the grade you earn. No whining about group dynamics when it's over. Under-stood?"

The three of them nodded.

"Second of all, Kevin, I know your parents are con-cerned about your English grade. They need to know that your A minus could become a B plus if the project grade isn't what you hope."

"Mrs. Mason: I hear you and I feel you," Kevin said.

"I'm only interested in you understanding me."

"Roger that."

"Excellent," Mr. Carrow said. "I'm excited to see what this professional writer comes up with."

Kevin beamed, but lost the smile when Mrs. Mason picked up his phone. "You know, Mr. Carrow, these cases are very slippery. Students drop them all the time, and the screens break fairly easily. It would be a shame, if—when taking this from Kevin during Resource because he chose to violate the phone policy in my room—it just . . . slipped out of my hand. My grip isn't what it used to be. Old age, I guess."

Kevin gulped.

Mr. Carrow was trying to hide a smirk. "A terrible shame."

Mrs. Mason handed Kevin his phone, but held on when he grabbed the other end. Oliver didn't see any issues with her grip. "Roger that, Kevin?"

"Roger that," he whispered.

CHAPTER TWENTY

BACKGROUND

"How's it going?" Ella asked from the couch. She dug her hand into a bowl of Cheez-Its like a backhoe and swung it up to her mouth.

"Good." Oliver finished rereading one of Stone's letters on his desktop computer. They'd been waging "Operation Find Some Compelling Background Information" for almost an hour. "I think I got something."

Kevin hopped up from his sprawled-out position on the carpet to the giant white butcher paper hanging on the wall. Ella had drawn a less crappy triangle that represented Private Stone's life story plot and filled in what they knew so far: Stone's enlistment in 1862 and (embarrassing) death at Gettysburg in 1863.

"Lay it on me," Kevin said.

"It's not really anything specific, just something Stone keeps talking about." Oliver did a keyword search for "Father" and picked out the first example.

"Like here: *Tell Father I do not regret my service. I know he thinks I acted foolishly.* And then later he says, *Tell Father I miss taking the wheat to Philadelphia with him and seeing the city.* And this one—from the deathbed letter Ella found: *He spoke often of his father, wanting him to know that he did not regret enlisting even though he never saw the battlefield.*"

"Sounds like he had some real daddy issues," Kevin said.

"Yeah—like his dad didn't want him to enlist or something." He tapped his finger on the mouse. "Did he have any brothers?"

Ella shuffled her notes. "Ancestry.com says he only had a sister. Why?"

"He was the only son . . . and he was almost twenty . . . so maybe he was supposed to take over the farm," Oliver said, stringing the ideas together as he said them. "But then he enlisted instead, which pissed off his dad, who was getting old. That would explain why he keeps bringing it up, right?"

"Ollie: That's brilliant."

Kevin started scribbling on the butcher paper. "Now *that* is some sweet background: A young wheat farmer, set to take over the family business, abandons tradition and heeds Lincoln's call to save the Union. He leaves his home, his parents, sister—girlfriend maybe, we'll see—unaware that he will be one of several hundred thousand to make the ultimate sacrifice. Boom."

"Wait—when I was at the historical society on Sunday I found this letter to Stone's dad that talks about a contract or something Stone made with this other guy," Oliver said. "Maybe it's related to why he enlisted in Philly."

Ella cut him a glance. "You went by yourself?"

"Yeah. What?"

"Nothing." She shrugged. "Does this contract thing really matter?"

"I'll let you know if I find out."

Ella leafed through her notes even though there wasn't any reason to. ". . . Okay."

"What?"

"I just think we should focus on the important stuff."

Rebellion rumbled in his gut. "I think this might be important."

"Okay," she said. Oliver thought it sounded more like a *whatever.*

Kevin sprawled out again and helped himself to another handful of Cheez-Its. "I'll start working that into the script, and you can search for tranquil farming photos for the opening sequence. Just google 'Lancaster' or 'Amish Country.' And maybe we can find some Civil War–era pictures of Doylestown. Then our background is set. No more awkward intro that leaves the viewer confused."

They worked in triumphant silence for a while.

"So your sister really likes the piano," Kevin said.

"I don't even notice it anymore," Oliver said. "Like if someone shaved your eyebrows. At first you'd notice, but then after a while you'd forget."

"That analogy is very specific and very strange," Kevin said. "I like it. Can I use it in a story?"

"Sure."

"Verbal contracts are binding in Pennsylvania, so make sure you're actually serious about this."

"You can use it."

"I think it's calming," Ella said. "The piano."

"A lot better than if I was up there," Kevin said. "My parents tried to get me to play a stringed instrument— you know, because we're Korean—so I picked the violin. They gave up after a few months when the neighbors thought I was slaughtering geese in my bedroom. Tried the bass next, but I kept dropping the thing. Turns out I'm not musical."

"Right. You're a writer," Ella said.

Kevin sucked his Capri Sun until it crinkled. "Sure."

Oliver could tell Kevin was holding something back. "Your parents don't know you write."

"Nope."

"Why not?" Ella asked.

"Because I never told them."

"What do they think you're doing on your phone all the time?" Oliver asked.

"Texting. And playing Clash of Clans."

"You should tell them," Ella said. "You write better than a lot of adults. I think they'd be really proud."

"That's because you're not Korean. If it's not math, science, or music, they don't care. You guys need to brush up on your Asian stereotypes. And I say that as a very proud Asian American."

Oliver looked at him sideways. Kevin sighed.

"Okay. You know what helicopter parents are, right?" Kevin threw his arms out and spun around. "Hovering above you all the time? That's what mine are like, except imagine that there are two helicopters and they both have missiles, and those missiles are expectations firing at you pretty much all the time: Kevin, you should be a mathlete; Kevin, you should play the violin; Kevin, why aren't you first in your Korean language class?"

"You take Korean?" Oliver asked.

"Tuesday nights."

Ella chewed on a nail. "At least you don't have satellite parents. And I don't mean NASA satellites that are always communicating with earth; I mean like the moon. Just a rock way out in space that sometimes you can't even see."

Oliver felt that weird tension fill the room again.

"Right—which is why you're tanking school," Kevin said. "I'm gonna be real with you, Ella: That whole thing confuses me. What's the endgame? Please tell me it doesn't end with you hitchhiking to California, because I saw this thing on TV about hitchhiking and it looked pretty dangerous."

Oliver made a *dude—seriously?* face.

"Oh, sorry," Kevin backtracked. "Not my biz—not my biz."

Ella reached for a Cheez-It. "I'm sending a message."

"What message?" Oliver asked.

"That I'm mad at them."

"Can't you just tell them?"

"No."

"How come?"

She looked at him like that was the dumbest question she'd ever been asked. "I shouldn't have to. They should just know—they're adults. They're smart enough to make tons of money, which they use to buy tons of stupid things, which they barely enjoy because they're too busy working."

Oliver let that sit for a few seconds. "It's a pretty serious message."

"It's a pretty serious thing."

Oliver pretended to be really into the drawing on the front of his Capri Sun.

"Does any of this have to do with . . . ya know," Kevin said. ". . . the hair . . . and . . . all that?"

An elephant of secondhand embarrassment sat on Oliver's chest; he couldn't move or breathe. He could only dread Ella's reaction.

Her flat stare morphed into a smirk. She tucked a strand of greasy hair behind her ear.

"Genius," Kevin said. "Stick it to 'em."

Oliver wasn't really clear on why Ella wouldn't just *tell* her parents what the heck was going on, but he didn't want to stick his nose in this mess. He just nodded and said, "Yeah. The man. Get him."

"That's the plan," Ella said.

CHAPTER TWENTY-ONE

THE SUBSTITUTE

"Hey," Oliver said to Hal.

Hal waved. Or maybe he was just putting more M&M's into his mouth. It was hard to tell. Oliver waved back anyway.

It was Wednesday and he didn't really have to be at the historical society. He wanted to be there. He wanted to figure out what that contract was. He needed to figure out why Stone enlisted in a regiment he shouldn't have.

"None of this makes sense," he said.

Hal spun around slowly in his chair.

"Sorry," Oliver said. "Just thinking aloud."

Hal downed some more M&M's.

Oliver opened up his mom's giant laptop from a time before laptops were a thing and reviewed his progress.

Why did Stone join the 68th?

    <u>Theory #3:</u> ???????

      • Find that contract thing

Oliver got the box of Stone documents off the shelf and began leafing through the binder.

And the first thing he found was two more letters from that H. Weller guy.

Philadelphia, Pennsylvania
May 13, 1863

Mr. Stone,
I pray my letter comes after Raymond's, so that he has the pleasure of sharing that our Lord has kept him safe from the carnage at Chancellorsville. If not, know that I have it on good authority that the 68th did not arrive in time to be tossed into the fray of battle. Raymond is alive, as I pray he stays.

Your humble servant,
H. Weller

"Why is this guy so worried about you dying?" Oliver asked Stone quietly.

Philadelphia, Pennsylvania
July 18, 1863

Mr. Stone,
It was with great sadness that I received your letter
regarding the passing of Raymond at Gettysburg.
My heart is grieved far more than I dare say to you,
his father, for your loss is beyond comparison. But
as the man whose place he took in battle, I must say
that I am deeply sorry for your loss.
*   I shall make arrangements to travel north Friday*
next to deliver the funds contracted between Raymond
and myself.

*   Your humble servant,*
*   H. Weller*

But as the man whose place he took in battle . . .

Oliver leaned in until the screen was an inch from
his face. He was back in the secret cave again, way
way up on the mountain. Except instead of a dead end,
Oliver could see the outline of a hidden door.

"A substitute," he said. "Holy crap."

Oliver clapped his hands together in a loud *smack*.

"You were a substitute for H. Weller. That's why you
enlisted down in Philly—because he was from Philly.

And the contract—he must have owed you money, but since you're dead it went to your family."

Hal turned around, glaring.

"Sorry," Oliver said. "Just uh, I figured out that thing I asked you about last week—why Stone enlisted in Philadelphia instead of his hometown. He did it because some rich guy named H. Weller got picked in the draft, and hired Stone to fight in his place."

Hal opened another packet of M&M's.

Then he said, "No."

"What?" Oliver said.

"The draft was in 1863. Private Raymond Stone enlisted in 1862."

Oliver blinked. "Oh. Right. I knew that."

Hal raised his eyebrows and spun back around.

Oliver stared at the letters. This didn't make sense. H. Weller literally said Stone took his place in battle, and there was all this talk about funds and a contract.

What.

The crap.

Oliver smelled chocolate. He looked up.

"Jeez."

Hal was standing right behind him.

"Have to lock up in ten minutes," Hal said.

"Okay. Let me uh, just text my mom and I'll put everything back."

Hal waddled to the back offices and Oliver stared at his progress. Or lack thereof. He knew H. Weller had paid Stone to fight in his place—which totally knocked Stone down another notch in Oliver's mind, if that was possible, because real soldiers fight for country, not cash. But he still didn't understand how that substitution fit into the real history of the Civil War. It was like somebody had cheated and gotten away with something.

"I'm going to figure this out," he told Stone, updating his research record. "Because no matter what Ella says, it's important. Details always are."

Theory #3: Stone enlisted in the 68th as a substitute for some guy named H. Weller.

How to prove:

• Find more letters from H. Weller

  • Figure out who H. Weller was

-CHAPTER TWENTY-TWO-
SAWBONES

"Ewww." Samantha wrinkled her face and looked away as Mr. Carrow buzzed into the room. "Why are you covered in blood?"

"Excellent question," Mr. Carrow said. "A related question might be: Why am I carrying a ten-inch bone saw—also covered in blood?" He swung the tool by Max's head and the kid ducked. "And what are all these bloody tools on the table? And this chest full of weird medical vials?"

"You're a Civil War surgeon," Oliver almost shouted.

"For that correct answer, I will not amputate your leg," Mr. Carrow said. "Let's go, people: Join me around the center table."

Oliver wormed his way next to Ella. "This is gonna be awesome. Let's get closer."

She didn't budge. "Is he allowed to even do this?"

"He's not going to actually amputate someone's leg."

"Still."

"Do you get queasy?"

"A little."

"Okay. We can stay back here."

"Gang, Civil War surgeons get a bad rep," Mr. Carrow said. "'Sawbones' or 'Butcher' were common nicknames for doctors like me who had to navigate the carnage of the battlefield. Based on my appearance, you could say that's fair. But remember this: The Germ Theory wasn't an accepted thing in 1861. Considering the technology they had, and the number of men these doctors had to work on, you could actually say that Civil War surgeons were pretty advanced." He set down the saw and wiped his hands on the bloody apron. "I need a volunteer."

A bunch of hands shot up, and Mr. Carrow picked Ian. "Lie down here; head at this end, feet down there."

Ian's head rested right near Samantha. "If I die," he said, "you can have all my stuff."

She giggled.

"The bad news, Ian, is that you've been shot in the leg," Mr. Carrow said. "Because of the giant, soft lead Minié balls fired from these new rifles, your shinbone has fragmented and sent shards up into your knee, along with bits of your super-dirty trousers." Mr. Carrow leaned down real close to Ian. "I can't save your knee; but I'm going to try and save your life."

"Mommy," Ian whined. The class snickered—except for Ella. Oliver noticed her face had absolutely zero color.

"The good news is that I'm a Union surgeon, which means I've got better supplies than my Confederate counterparts." Mr. Carrow opened the wooden chest and took out a vial and cloth. "Ether was the most common form of anesthesia; 'biting the bullet' to endure the pain wasn't really a thing. Doctors would douse the cloth like this," he said, soaking the rag and placing it over Ian's mouth, "and the patient would inhale until he passed out."

Ian went slack.

"It's just water, people," Mr. Carrow said. More laughs. "Now that he's under, I need to prep the leg." He wrapped what looked like a thick leather bracelet around Ian's thigh and turned a crank knob until it got tight.

"He's cutting off blood to the wound," Oliver told Ella.

She wasn't looking. "Uh-huh."

"If you actually can't feel your leg anymore, say something," Mr. Carrow told Ian.

Ian saluted.

"Notice how I'm not washing my hands," Mr. Carrow said, rinsing the tools in a murky basin of water.

"I've done a dozen surgeries already and will do a dozen more. Speed is the goal: The longer I take with Ian, the sooner another wounded soldier might die." He grabbed a pair of large hooknose pliers and began digging around on Ian's knee. "I'll pick out any bone fragments and pieces of cloth—the bullet if I'm lucky—before making my mark for amputation. Max, hand me that scalpel. I need to cut a flap of skin on both sides to wrap around the bone after I cut off the leg."

Half the class wailed at that. Ella scooched back, totally out of the group.

"Are you okay?" Oliver asked.

Her face was on its way to green. "Fine."

He got her a chair and she sat. "You want to get a drink or something?"

"It's okay, I'm fine. Go watch."

"I can see from here." Oliver stood on a chair.

"I'm cutting through the skin," Mr. Carrow said, "and when I reach the bone it's time to get down to business." He grabbed the saw. "An experienced surgeon would hack off a limb in about ten minutes. I'm not saying it was pretty, but it was efficient. Ian, pray that I gave you enough ether. Also, you might want to just generally pray. Survival rate is about fifty-fifty at this point."

Ian moaned.

Mr. Carrow did one pass with the saw and the room erupted in terror; Oliver could see he was grinding the saw against a piece of wood, but it sounded like it was actually cutting through bone.

"This is awesome," Oliver said.

Ella put her head on the table.

"Hey." Oliver jumped off the chair. "I'm going to tell him you're feeling sick."

"No. It's fine."

"And because I'm in a rush," Mr. Carrow yelled over the groans, "I'm just going to toss this leg into a pile of other legs underneath the table. Clunk. Bye-bye leg. Oh no—it rolled off the pile of legs. Tara, pick up Ian's leg, would you?"

"Let's at least ask to go in the hall," Oliver said.

Ella squeezed her eyes shut. "I'm kind of dizzy. I'll just wait."

"Now, before I sew up the wound, I've got to file down the bone so it doesn't poke through the skin," Mr. Carrow said. He took a file and rubbed it against the wood fragment. More squeals. "Max, hand me that needle. Okay. The trick is to grab the flaps of skin, take my needle and silk—or in the Confederate Army, boiled horsehair—and stitch it shut. Later in the war surgeons figured out that bromine, a very caustic chemical, killed the bacteria that caused gangrene, so I'd sprinkle some of that on the leg too."

Ella let out a soft moan.

"That's it," Oliver said. "I'm telling him—"

The unmistakable sound of someone puking their guts cut through the noisy room.

Max, the surgical assistant, had just vomited all over Ian.

"AHHHHH," Ian shrieked. *"AHHHHHHHHHH!"*

The room went insane. Another student gagged; more screaming. Mr. Carrow ran to the storage cabinet for paper towels and started giving directions.

"Ian—help Max to the bathroom."

"HE JUST PUKED ON ME—"

"I know, and that's insanely gross, but you'll survive. Walk him to the bathroom, clean him up, and then take him to the nurse."

Ian looked down at his puke-covered shirt. He looked up at Samantha, who backed away.

"Listen up, gang," Mr. Carrow shouted. "We're going to get some air in the courtyard while I call the janitor. If you feel sick, tell somebody, and have them walk next to you. Last thing we need is a concussion from one of you keeling over."

"Can you walk?" Oliver asked Ella.

"I think so."

"Stay here for a second; I'll grab our stuff."

Oliver scampered through the exiting crowd to Ella's desk and grabbed her binder. His was by the door, so he figured he could get it on the way out. He'd carry both binders in one arm, to keep the other free in case—

From across the room he saw Ella stand up. She swayed like a ship finding balance on the other side of a giant swell. She righted herself for a second, but then another wave came.

She was going down.

Oliver moved faster than he'd ever moved in his life. It was like a movie—everything slowed down. Dropping his binder, he leaped over a chair and shoved past the crowd. Ella was falling fast—too fast for him to stop her.

He'd have to break the fall.

Sliding to his knees, Oliver aimed for a spot and stretched out his arms.

CHAPTER TWENTY-THREE

KEVIN SPEAKS
(ABOUT THE PROBLEMS OF
DATING PEOPLE YOU WORK WITH)

"I'm going to have a talk with Mr. Carrow after school," Mrs. Bilker said. "You're the third one today. Keep drinking."

Ella shifted up a little on the cot and took another sip from the bottle. Oliver thought she looked better, but still pale.

"And you're sure she didn't hit her head?" Mrs. Bilker asked Oliver.

"Nope."

"You're sure."

"Positive."

"Because concussions are very serious."

"Ollie caught her," said Max from two cots down. He looked better too—less barfy. "Like in the movies. It was pretty awesome."

"Caught her?"

Max put his arms out like a cradle.

"Good for you, Oliver. Saved Ella some potential brain damage and me a week of paperwork."

"Friends don't let friends crack their heads open on school grounds, I guess," Ella said.

Oliver's face burned like a wildfire, but his chest swelled with pride. He'd done something truly awesome—truly *heroic.*

So why was he nervous?

The nurse's office door swung open and Kevin scuttled in. "Good afternoon, Nurse Bilker."

"Like I've told you before, Kevin, *Mrs.* Bilker is fine. The 'nurse' is implied."

"I consider it a sign of respect to address you by your official title." He looked around to survey the wounded. "Some crazy stories are flying around the cafeteria. Did Max really barf on Ian?"

"Affirmative," Max mumbled.

"And Ollie dove across a table to keep Ella from dying?"

"I didn't dive across a table."

"But he jumped over a chair." Max grimaced and rubbed his stomach. "S'mores Pop-Tarts are kind of ruined for me now."

"I think you might have ruined them for some

other people too," Mrs. Bilker said. The phone rang and she picked up. "Nurse's office. . . . Okay. Thanks, I'll walk him down." She hung up. "Your mom's here, Max."

"S'mores was the best flavor." Max grunted as he shouldered his bag. Oliver smelled a little bit of barf as he walked by. "See ya, guys."

"See ya."

Kevin plopped onto the rolling stool and wheeled over to Ella's cot. "It's pretty cool—this whole saving thing."

"I didn't—"

Kevin held up a hand. "It's pretty cool. I'm just warning you: Romance can railroad a group project pretty fast. Lots of emotional carnage."

"Uh." Oliver tried to play it cool and leaned against Mrs. Bilker's desk. "What?"

"You know." Kevin wagged a finger between them. "*You* know."

Ella shrunk lower into the cot.

"I mean, it's fine if you're gonna go out," Kevin said, "but I think you should know what you're getting into. First, you'll always be trying to maneuver the seating arrangement so you're next to each other, and I'll have to pretend I don't know what's happening when I really do. Then you'll be staring into each other's eyes and we'll never get any work done. Then you'll be meeting up without me to make out."

Half of Oliver's butt cheek slipped off the desk. He barely caught himself in time to avoid a full-on wipeout.

"And then if you break up, things will get super awkward. You'll both start bailing on group meetings. The documentary could suffer. Ella might fail social studies and be doomed to repeat seventh grade. Worst of all, I'll be back in Mason's Resource choking on her perfume."

"Kevin," Oliver said. He had to shut the kid up. "We're just friends."

"You know who else was just friends? Everybody who's ever gone out."

"We get it," Ella said. "Nobody goes out with anybody."

"Whoa, whoa," Kevin said. "Let's not get crazy here. I was just shooting up some flares. You two can do whatever you want. I mean, this is America."

"We get it," Oliver said. The words came out fast and jumbled. He just wanted to get the heck out of there. "For the sake of the project."

Kevin gave a big nod, like he'd said his piece, and headed for the door.

He was gone for only a second before he popped back.

"Just checking to make sure you weren't making out yet."

A few seconds of silence went by after he left.

"That was . . . weird," Oliver said.

"Yeah."

Oliver cut her a quick glance.

"Uh, okay," Oliver said. "I should probably go to lunch."

"Okay."

He heard a hitch in her voice. "I mean, unless you want me to . . . stay."

Ella was kind of pale again, and shaking a little. "Would you mind?"

The hero feeling was back.

"Friends don't let friends sit alone in the nurse's office," he said.

CHAPTER TWENTY-FOUR

THE SCORECARD
OF EMOTIONS

"No, I do not need any assistance," Oliver told the annoying customer service chat box that kept popping up on every page of the Weller Bank's website on his basement computer. It was one of the few good leads that came up when he googled "H. Weller," but the chat box kept popping up every time he tried to click around on his own, and it gave him *nothing* when he asked it about H. Weller. It was like a brick wall.

"I will not have a good day," he told the customer service chat supporter.

Oliver went back to his Word doc.

Theory #3: Stone enlisted in the 68th as a substitute for some guy named H. Weller.

<u>How to prove:</u>

- Find more letters from H. Weller
  - Find out who H. Weller was
    - ~~Google the crap out of him~~
    - Search on Ancestry.com

After logging in with Ella's free trial account, Oliver entered "Weller" in the last name field and got a bagillion records. Most of them came from census data, which was basically when America counted all of the people every ten years. Oliver narrowed the search to males from the 1860s who had ever lived in Philadelphia, which helped bring the number down a little.

To three hundred and sixteen.

"Well, crap," Oliver said.

He scrolled through lots of Jesses and Johns and some guy named Fride until he realized he could filter for anybody whose name started with *H*. That narrowed it down to sixteen.

Exactly.

Oliver scanned to the bottom.

"Hello, Henry."

The Ancestry card didn't have anything other than his wife's and son's names, so Oliver went back to Google—this time, with a first name.

And again, the first hit was the Weller Financial Group.

A chat box popped up asking how they could be of service.

"You could tell me who Henry Weller is," Oliver typed in with 100 percent sarcasm.

It paused for a few seconds. Then, at last, it spit out a real answer.

Henry Weller is the former president of the Weller Bank, the forerunner to the Weller Financial Group. Here is a link to a brief history of his role in the company.

Oliver blinked.

He followed the link to the company's "About Us" page.

The Weller Financial Group traces its origins to nineteenth-century America. Thomas Weller, a wealthy businessmen and prominent member of the Society of Friends, founded the Weller Bank on 7th and Chestnut Streets in 1848. Generous lending practices and low interest rates quickly made the bank a favorite among Philadelphian merchants and farmers. In 1871, Thomas's eldest son, Henry Weller, took over as bank president, a position he held until his death in 1938.

Oliver breathed out.

<u>Theory #3:</u> Stone enlisted in the 68th as a substitute for some guy named H. Weller.

<u>How to prove:</u>

- Find more letters from H. Weller
    - Find out who H. Weller was
        - ~~Google the crap out of him~~
        - Search on Ancestry.com
            - Weller Bank president was also named Henry Weller (says so on their website)
            - Find out if this is the same H. Weller who wrote Stone's dad those letters

Oliver's phone buzzed.

Ella. *Hey.*

Oliver googled "Why does my stomach feel weird when this girl texts me" and got back a bunch of scary medical conditions.

Hey, he texted back.

I never said thx. For the fainting thing.

Oliver's chest swelled. It had been pretty awesome.

No prob, he texted.

☺

And I swear on a Bible that I won't ask you to go out with me.

He instantly regretted hitting SEND.

No response from Ella.

"Great," he said to the empty basement. He threw his phone on the couch. "Just great."

Oliver wandered upstairs and ate six Oreos at the breakfast bar. It was mostly quiet because Addie had piano lessons. The only sound was his dad watching *Seinfeld* reruns in the living room. Oliver looked at the half-eaten sleeve; it looked lonely, so he finished the rest and washed it down with a giant glass of milk, then walked into the living room.

His dad woke from a half nap. "Hey bud," he said. "What's up?"

"Nothing."

It was an early episode Oliver had seen a dozen times—when the storylines and acting hadn't been as funny, but you could tell it was going to be in the future. Oliver loved it.

"I have a question about girls."

The La-Z-Boy retracted as Oliver's dad sat up. "Um— well . . . great. Okay. Where to start—"

"Not that. Basic stuff. Like: How do you tell if you want to be . . . not friends with a girl. More than friends."

"You mean, if you like them?"

"Uh, yeah."

Oliver's dad lowered the volume. He looked a lot more relaxed now that he knew the conversation wouldn't involve basic anatomy. "Okay. There's usually some signs."

"Signs."

"Yeah. For example: When you see her, what do you feel like? Excited? Happy? Nervous? Or nothing—like when you see Mom."

"Let's leave Mom out of this."

"Right."

Oliver thought about the question. "I guess . . . happy. I like hanging out with her. She's nice and pretty cool."

"Hmm. That could go in the 'Friends' or 'More Than Friends' column. Let's put it in both for now."

Oliver thought some more. "Sometimes excited and nervous. Like when she texts me."

"Texting with a friend shouldn't make you nervous. I'd say that goes in the 'More Than Friends' column."

"Columns. So it's like a scorecard. Of emotions."

"I guess you could say that."

"And I just keep doing this with everything and then whichever one has the most will be the situation I'm in?"

His dad nodded. "Sometimes not feeling something is just as important as what you're feeling."

Oliver wished the anatomy talk with his mom had been this clear-cut.

"If the results say 'More Than Friends,' what do I do then?"

His dad laughed. "Ollie, you've just stumbled upon one of life's great questions."

"And?"

"And the answer is: It's complicated."

"Anything more concrete? I'm kinda in a . . . a situation."

"I've been in a few situations myself, you know. The last one was with your mother."

"I was pretty clear on Mom not being in this conversation."

"Sorry." His dad rubbed the stubble on his face. "At some point you have to just go for it."

Oreos and milk sloshed in Oliver's stomach at that scenario. He really shouldn't have eaten that whole sleeve. "So I just go up to her and say, 'I like you'? That sounds like a terrible idea. If she doesn't like me back, I'll look like an idiot."

"But at least you'll know."

Oliver wasn't so sure that was worth the risk. "My friend Kevin says that going out with someone you work with causes problems. He says it has a negative impact on product quality. Do you think that's true?"

"Maybe . . . but the tension could still be there. When you like someone a lot, it can be hard to spend a lot of time with them and not actually be *with* them, you know?"

Oliver thought about sitting with Ella in the nurse's office, and how all he wanted to do was stay there until she felt better. Where did that go on the scorecard?

Seinfeld came back from commercial and they watched for a minute.

"Okay. Thanks, Dad."

"You got it, bud. Let me know how things progress."

"Uh-huh."

Oliver went back down to the basement and eyed his phone from across the room. Had she thought his joke was funny or stupid? And why did he care so much?

Finally, he picked it up and looked at the screen.

☺

"Now what," he said, "does that mean?"

And then he opened up a new Word doc.

<u>Friends</u>

1. I think she's cool
2. I think she's nice
3. I like hanging out with her
4. I wanted to keep her from getting a concussion
5. I didn't want to leave her alone in the nurse's office

<u>More Than Friends</u>

1. I think she's cool
2. I think she's nice
3. I like hanging out with her
4. I wanted to keep her from getting a concussion
5. I didn't want to leave her alone in the nurse's office
6. I get nervous/excited when she texts me.

Oliver swallowed as he reviewed the data, which actually made him feel better because he could then add "Get nervous when the scorecard tells me I want to be more than friends with her" to the "Friends" column, because why would he be nervous unless he just wanted to be friends?

Okay. So it was a tie.

Which meant he needed more data.

-CHAPTER TWENTY-FIVE-
DATA COLLECTION

"I think he's eaten like five hundred M&M's since we got here," Kevin whispered to Oliver.

"Uh-huh."

Oliver was too busy fighting a migraine to deal with Hal's weirdness right now. And that was his own fault, really, because he'd offered to read letters *with* Ella instead of just type for her. The plan had been to be around her as much as possible so he could input more data into his Scorecard of Emotions and arrive at a clear conclusion.

But after three hours of reading Stone's scribbles, he actually needed her help less and less, until they weren't talking at all. He had a throbbing headache and absolutely zero new data for his Scorecard of Emotions.

"I can't believe they played baseball in camp," Ella said, putting away a letter Stone had sent to his mom. "With bases and bats and everything. That is so cool.

Makes me kinda sad Stone was so sick he couldn't even play."

Or maybe he was in his tent, counting his substitution cash, Oliver thought. "Most of my letters were about the weather and food and news about the war he heard from other camps."

Ella nodded like that was awesome. "This will be a great addition to the documentary—really play up the camp life angle."

"Uh-huh."

"I could go for some M&M's right now," Kevin said. "I wonder how he feels about sharing."

"I can guess," Oliver said.

Kevin went back to his script. Oliver typed the last sentence on his mom's clunky laptop and put the letter sleeve back into the three-ring binder. His eyes burned like someone had forced him to stare into the sun for an hour.

He looked at Ella and cleared his throat.

"What's wrong?" she asked.

"Huh?"

"You look like someone is standing on your stomach."

"That's it, I'm asking him," Kevin said. He walked across the room to Hal and stuck his hand out. "Kevin Kim: Pleased to meet you. This may sound kinda weird because we don't really know each other, but I see that you've got quite a lot of—"

Hal reached into his pocket and gave Kevin a bag of M&M's.

". . . Thanks."

Hal gave Kevin two more bags and pointed to Oliver and Ella. "For them."

". . . Wow, thanks Hal."

"Yes."

Kevin blinked. And for some reason did a little bow.

"That wasn't how I saw that happening," he whispered when he got back.

"I like sharing," Hal said.

"He has really good hearing," Oliver whispered.

"Yes," Hal said.

Whispering was clearly out.

"We're taking good care of the documents," Oliver said to Hal. "Right, Ella?"

She was lost in another letter. ". . . Yeah . . ."

"It's easier to see if you take it out," Hal said. "No glare. But you need these." He put his hand on the box of latex gloves.

"Can you make a copy of this letter?" Ella asked Hal.

"No."

She frowned. "Why not?"

"Light damages the documents."

Oliver's phone pinged. A text from his mom: *Ollie, I will be there in five minutes . . . please be outside so I can just pull up and don't have to beep . . . if you're not outside I will beep until you come out . . . Love you . . . Mom.*

"My mom's almost here," he said. "We should pack up."

Ella had buried herself in her notes. "Gotta focus. Quiet."

"I have to go to the bathroom. Kevin, will you go out to the car and meet her before she starts—"

Beeeeeeeeeeeeeeeeeeeeeeeep-beeeeeeep-beep.

"Crap, she's early," Oliver said. "Kevin, go tell her we're just finishing something so she stops beeping."

"Leaving me alone with all the M&M's is going to end with you having zero M&M's," Kevin said.

Beeeeep-beeeeeeeeeeeeeeeeep.

"You can have mine," Oliver said.

"No backsies."

"Whatever."

"No backsies is a serious, binding contract that has kept humans from backing out of agreements for thousands of years—"

Beeeeeeeeeeeeeeeeeeeeeeeeeeeeeeep.

"Fine—no backsies."

Kevin grabbed his stuff and ran out. Oliver stopped

by the bathroom and met Ella back at their table.

"Anything good?" he asked

But Ella didn't answer. She was staring at her phone like it had committed murder. "Dresses suck." Ella said the words out loud as she texted. She pushed the screen to black and shoved the phone in her pocket.

"Uh," Oliver said. "What?"

"My sister is coming home from college this week and wants to take me shopping for a stupid dress to wear to the spring dance," Ella explained as they walked out. "Which I'm not going to because dresses suck and dances suck."

"Right," Oliver said, but not because he agreed. He was too busy picturing Ella in a dress, in the gym, walking toward him in slow motion as an overhead disco ball covered her with glittering lights.

There was only one place on the scorecard for *that*.

Which meant it was official.

He liked her.

CHAPTER TWENTY-SIX

THE LOVE NOTE

"*Fix bayonets,*" Sergeant Tom ordered.

Oliver unhooked the long, sharp piece of metal from his utility belt and slipped it over the rifle. *Shunk.* It was easier doing it like this—crouched down behind picnic tables meant to represent a stone wall—than standing in formation.

"*CHARGE!*"

Oliver screamed at the top of his lungs as the 104th Pennsylvania Volunteers clambered up and over the tables. He tuned out the grunts and groans of his fellow soldiers and focused on the bottom of the hill, where a line of trees was standing in for Confederate soldiers.

He charged down the hill, legs pounding, lungs on fire. He was doing it—he was leading the infamous charge of Union soldiers down Little Round Top. Maybe Sergeant Tom would tell the guy in charge of the reenactment how good Oliver was, and he'd be the first one down the actual Little Round Top at Gettysburg in July. According to just about every Civil War historian, the defense of Little Round Top at Gettysburg had been the most critical Union counterattack of the three-day battle. Heroes had been made on that hill.

The sun ripped through a cloud and glinted off Oliver's bayonet. He thrust the rifle out. He screamed.

And then he fell.

Suddenly he was tumbling and eating dirt and all he could focus on was trying to avoid impaling himself on the bayonet.

Somehow he stopped rolling without getting stabbed.

"Ollie!" shouted Ella.

"That was bad," Kevin said, right behind her. "Ambulance-bad."

"Ollie—are you okay?"

"Ugh." Oliver squinted up at her. Maybe it was the sun, or maybe he was concussed, but it looked like a hundred suns were lighting her up. She looked kind of like an angel.

"Is he hurt?" shouted Sergeant Tom from the top of the hill.

"My shoulder kills," Oliver mumbled.

"The ground killed his shoulder," Kevin yelled back.

Ella dropped her project binder and helped Oliver

up. "I was really worried you were going to get stabbed by your own bayonet."

"Me too." Her being so worried about him took away some of the horrible embarrassment of falling.

Some.

"At least you made it close to enemy lines," Kevin said.

Sergeant Tom lumbered over. "That was some charge, Ollie. From the way you went down, I thought you actually got shot." Sergeant Tom held up a large orange cone. "Then I saw this. It was lying sideways, probably left by those Ultimate Frisbee players. You tripped right over it. Can you walk?"

"Yeah." Oliver took a step to feel things out. "This is all really embarrassing."

Ella laughed a little and brushed a few pieces of grass off his forehead. His entire face was suddenly on fire.

"I think the others will be in shape by July," Sergeant Tom said. Most of the 104th Pennsylvania Volunteers had stopped on the slope to relax. Some had never made it over the picnic tables.

"You sure about that, Sergeant?" Kevin asked.

"I guess as in shape as they're going to be. Sure you're okay, Oliver?"

"I'm good." Oliver glanced at Ella, but she was staring at her phone. "Sorry about getting your gun dirty."

"Eh, no problem." Sergeant Tom looked at his watch. "Almost noon. Guess I should dismiss. *Dismissed!*" he yelled up the hill. "See ya next week. We'll be back over by the pavilion. Check your email for changes."

Ella looked up from her phone. "My mom's here," she said. Oliver saw that look of murder in her eyes again. She stood up. "I'll see you guys on Monday."

"She seems mad," Kevin said as she walked away. "Please tell me you two aren't in some weird fight that I'm going to have to fix."

"Her sister is making her go dress shopping for the dance, but she doesn't want to go," Oliver said.

"She must be really pissed if she left that." Kevin pointed at her binder, lying on the ground. Oliver sighed and picked it up.

They joined the stragglers on a dirt path that led through the woods back to the parking lot. When they reached the pavilion, Oliver took off his forage cap and coat and lay down on the cool cement while Kevin did some script edits. Oliver's shoulder throbbed, but he was hurting way worse from general shame. He must've looked like a gigantic idiot falling down that hill. A wool-trousered idiot.

"How bad was the fall?" Oliver asked.

"Oh, terrible for sure. The kind of thing that would go viral on YouTube, but not in a good way."

"Great."

"It also proved that I was right about you two."

Oliver sat up. "What do you mean?"

"She was in an all-out sprint down that hill to see if you were hurt."

"I guess," Oliver said. "But so were you. Friends don't just sit there while their friends maybe impale themselves."

"Friends don't gently brush grass off their friend's face," Kevin said. "And don't even get me started on how she dresses prettier when she comes to drill. Not that I'm interested—I've got my eye on a very interesting sixth grader. Sort of a free spirit. Apparently she can talk to birds."

"Uh-huh."

"What I'm saying is, it's pretty clear that she likes you, so you can stop being all weird that you like her."

"I never said I like her."

"Are we telling jokes now?" Kevin raised his eyebrows and started typing again.

Oliver rubbed his shoulder. There was no way Ella liked him back.

But maybe there was a way to be sure.

He flipped open her binder to a clump of lined paper and made her a scorecard:

Friends	More Than Friends
1. She likes to hang out with me.	1. She likes to hang out with me.
2. She ran really fast to see if I was hurt	2. She ran really fast to see if I was hurt
	3. She wears pretty clothes when she comes to watch me drill.
	4. She brushed grass off my face.

It was a start.

Oliver took his paper out of the rings and flipped everything back slowly to shut the binder because everybody knows there are few things more annoying than making a giant logjam in there that requires you to take every paper out.

That's when he saw it: a note.

In Ella's handwriting.

He started to read it but stopped. He looked over at Kevin. Still buried in his script edits.

This was what people called an invasion of privacy. Completely inappropriate. Maybe illegal. He could go to jail, which was terrifying, because from everything he'd seen on TV, he was the kind of person who wouldn't do well in jail.

But she'd never know. And was it really that bad? She *had* left the binder. He was basically doing her a favor by rescuing it. He deserved to read the note.

So he read it.

I see you when I close my eyes because you've been by my side the last few days. I have never said what I am about to say to anyone, and I am embarrassed to say it to you. I suppose I should just say it before I lose my nerve or run out of time. I love you.

"Bro," Kevin said.

Oliver couldn't get enough air into his lungs. "Huh?"

"You okay? You look like you're gonna puke."

"I what?"

Kevin stared at him. "Sure you didn't bayonet yourself in the head?"

"Uh—no. I'm fine. Just . . . my shoulder. It hurts."

Beeeeeeeeeeeeeep-beeeeeeeeeeep.

"Your mom really loves that horn," Kevin said. "Are you gonna tell her what happened?"

Oliver's brain was mush.

I love you.

Those words had fried the circuitry upstairs.

"Tell her what?" Oliver asked.

"You know, when you tripped over that cone and

did like ten somersaults down the hill?"

"Oh . . . right. Uh, no. Let's keep that between us."

"Okay." Kevin looked Oliver over. "I think you should see a doctor."

Beeeeeep-beeeeeeeeeeeeeeeeeeeeep-beeeeeeep.

In the car, Oliver waited until Kevin was buried back in the script before he added "wrote me a love note" to Ella's "More Than Friends" column.

It was official, then.

They liked each other.

–CHAPTER TWENTY-SEVEN–
VENTI CHAI TEA LATTE—DIRTY—NO WATER, EXTRA HOT, WITH FIVE PUMPS OF VANILLA SYRUP

Oliver decided to finally send the text at 9:42 the next morning.

Hey. You left your binder at the park. Want me to drop it off?

He left out the part about rereading her love note seven hundred times.

That's okay. I can get it at school, she texted back.

You don't live that far. I can just ride my bike over.

I'm not at home. I'm at Starbucks with my dad.

Oh. Cool.

Not really.

?

?

Oliver wasn't sure where to go from there.

And then suddenly he knew exactly where to go.

He made his hair look not terrible and bounded upstairs. "Dad, I need a ride to Starbucks."

His mom looked over her cup of coffee. "Why?"

He held up the binder. "Ella left this at the park and needs it for the project."

"Can't you just give it to her tomorrow?"

"I could . . ." Oliver said, looking to his dad for help.

"But the project might suffer," his dad finished. "You know what—I need to get some propane for the grill anyway. We can drop it off on the way."

Five minutes later they were in the van heading toward the shopping center.

"I guess your . . . situation . . . has moved forward," his dad said.

"Uh, yeah."

"Need any first date advice?"

Oliver sucked in his gut. "It's not a date. I'm just dropping this off."

Weird dad smile that meant something. "Maybe you're smoother than I thought."

"I am the opposite of smooth. I'm just giving her the binder."

They pulled into the shopping center and slowed outside Starbucks. "Send me a text if you need backup."

"Uh-huh." Oliver spotted Ella and her dad through the window; she was reading, and he was on his laptop in front of him. Suddenly Oliver wondered if this was a terrible idea.

He shook his head. He wiped his sweaty palms on his jeans.

He just had to go for it.

Oliver had never been in a Starbucks before. His parents were more make-your-coffee-at-home people. The slow rock music and burnt coffee smell were weird. He walked over to Ella.

"Hi."

She didn't look up from her book.

"Yes," Mr. Berry said.

Oliver shifted from foot to foot. Maybe Ella's scorecard was wrong. "I'm just here to give this to Ella." He held out the binder to Mr. Berry. "She left it at the—"

"Nope," Mr. Berry said.

"Yeah," Oliver said, "she dropped it yesterday."

"Adam, hold on, would you?" Mr. Berry turned his head toward Oliver. "Oh—hey. Oliver. What's up?"

Oliver saw the Bluetooth device in Mr. Berry's other ear. "Uh—sorry, I didn't know you were on the phone. Ella left this at the park and I was just dropping it off."

"Ella," her dad said. No response. This was worse

than falling down the hill. He was impaling himself on his own stupidity. "Ella, baby." Mr. Berry tapped her book.

Ella glared at him through her hair. "What?"

Mr. Berry pointed at Oliver.

Ella took out her earbuds buried in her hair.

Oh.

"Hey," Oliver said. He held out the stupid freaking binder again. "I was running errands with my dad and thought I'd just drop this off."

"Thanks."

Oliver had expected her to be a little more happy/impressed/anything. He hadn't really planned what to do next.

So he just stood there.

Awkwardly.

"Do you want to sit down?" Mr. Berry asked.

"Why, so he can listen to you and your buddies talk about money?" Ella asked. "I'm pretty sure Oliver would rather be dead."

Mr. Berry's mouth opened, but nothing came out. He took the Bluetooth out of his ear and sipped his coffee. He looked a little sad, actually.

Ella got up and walked to the bathroom.

Mr. Berry and Oliver stared at each other.

"I almost bayoneted myself yesterday," Oliver said.

Nothing like the story of his greatest humiliation to fill the silence. "It was my own bayonet. That was the most embarrassing part. And the falling down the hill."

". . . Sorry to hear that. Are you okay?"

"Yeah. That's why Ella forgot the binder. She came over to make sure I wasn't hurt."

"She can be very kind, when she wants to be."

Oliver felt like he'd wandered into a conversation he shouldn't be in.

Ella came back to the table and gathered her stuff. "I'll be in the car."

"Ella." Mr. Berry said her name like he was tiptoeing around a landmine. "Oliver came all this way to give you your binder. Why don't you get him something to drink?"

"It's fine," Oliver said. Ella didn't seem happy to see him. Did he misread the love note somehow? "My dad's just over at Sears getting some propane. I gotta go anyway."

"Get something to go." Mr. Berry took out some cash and gave it to Ella. "Come on—don't be rude."

Ella took the money.

"Let's go," she muttered at Oliver.

He followed her to the line. "Uh, sorry—about this."

Ella glanced over at her dad, who was back on the

Bluetooth. She looked down at the cash in her hand. "Ollie, I have a very serious question for you."

Oliver swallowed. Was she going to ask him to go out? Was he even ready for this level of commitment?

"Do you like lattes?"

He blinked. "Huh?"

"Lattes," Ella said. "Do you like them?"

"Uh, I don't know. I never had one."

"It's milk and coffee with tons of sugar and hot steam shot through it."

"Sounds pretty good."

"Oh, it's incredible."

"Next," the barista called out.

"Two Venti Chai Tea Lattes—dirty—no water, extra hot, with five pumps of vanilla syrup," Ella ordered.

The barista wrote the order details on each cup with a Sharpie. ". . . Did you say five—"

"Yes—five pumps of vanilla syrup."

"And a shot of espresso in each."

"Yes."

"That's going to be—"

"Really expensive. I know."

The barista rung up the total and blinked. "Twenty-four thirty-five."

"Twenty-four dollars?" Oliver said. "That's like a month's supply of Capri Suns at my house."

"Here's fifty," Ella said. "Keep the change."

Ella stalked over to the far counter and folded her arms tightly.

"Isn't your dad going to be upset?" Oliver asked. He had never even seen a fifty-dollar bill before.

"Who cares? He deserves it."

"For what?"

Ella nodded toward her dad, who was hunched over his laptop concentrating really hard. "That—the nonstop working. Ignoring life and everybody in it."

He saw tears gather under her eyes. Should Oliver hug her? He had no scorecard for this.

Who knew these things?

"They talk about two things: Charlie and money. And he brings me here like we're on some father-daughter outing and he *works*. It's completely *inane*."

"Insane?"

"In-*ane*. It means silly and stupid."

"Right."

"Two Venti Chai Tea Lattes—dirty—no water, extra hot, with five pumps of vanilla syrup," the barista called out. Oliver wondered if you had to have a degree in made-up languages to work there.

Ella handed Oliver one of the gigantic drinks and tapped her cup against his. "Cheers."

Oliver took a sip. "Holy crap."

"Good, right?"

"Incredible."

Ella grinned.

She walked over to the trash can, hovered the drink over the top for a second, and then dropped it in.

CHAPTER TWENTY-EIGHT

THE FIRST EMAIL

To: info@wellergroupfinancial.org
Subject: Henry Weller

Dear Weller Group people,

My name is Oliver Prichard and I'm a seventh grader at Kennesaw Middle School. I'm doing a social studies project about a Civil War soldier from my town, and I discovered something I think relates to your company and former bank president Henry Weller.

Basically, my theory is that Henry Weller paid the soldier I'm studying, Private Raymond Stone, to enlist in his place with the 68th Pennsylvania Volunteer Regiment in 1862. I don't really know if that's even possible, because the draft didn't exist that early in the war, so paid substitution definitely didn't. The only thing I have to prove this is a few letters, which

I scanned and attached for you to check out. What I'd like to know is if you have any family records of this happening, or could give me any information at all to confirm that the Henry Weller who wrote my letters is the same Henry Weller who took over as president of your bank in 1871.

I'm sure this probably sounds a little crazy, but I promise I'm not like a scammer or anything. Although I bet that probably happens a lot because you have a lot of money being a bank and all.

Anyway, I'm sure you're probably really busy, but I'd love for you to check it out and let me know if you find anything. The project is due in a week and I'm kind of under a deadline and my friend who's helping needs to get a hundred or she might have to repeat seventh grade. But no rush.

Thanks for reading this. Have a nice day.

From,
Oliver Prichard

CHAPTER TWENTY-NINE

THE IMPORTANCE
OF CONTEXT

Oliver pushed through the overgrown brush along the path to school. He couldn't stop thinking about the letter. He'd definitely read it right. It definitely said "I love you."

In all the confusion, he'd completely forgotten the H. Weller discovery. It wasn't until ten at night that Oliver had gone back to his research and decided to email the Weller Group to see if they could maybe confirm that their bank president after the Civil War, Henry Weller, was the H. Weller that Stone substituted for.

Maybe love made you forget stuff.

Who knew these things.

After third period Oliver raced to the computer lab to make sure they got their spot up front, far from other computers in case there was any sensitive dialogue.

"Hey," he said when she sat down.

"About yesterday," Ella said. "Sorry I was in such a bad mood."

"It's okay." Oliver picked at the fraying corners of his binder. "And sorry about your dad ignoring you and everything."

"Yeah. Sucks."

Awkward silence.

"So other than, uh, Starbucks, did you have a good weekend?"

"Not really. My sister came home from college Friday and made me go shopping with her to buy that stupid dress."

"Oh right," he said. "Did you get one?"

"Yeah."

"How come?"

"Because the dance is this Saturday."

"I thought you weren't going?" Oliver asked.

"It's complicated."

"Okay." Oliver messed with the screen brightness on his monitor. "So who you gonna go with?"

She shrugged.

Oliver swallowed. Was this his moment? Should he go for it? Was she waiting for him to go for it?

"I'm going by myself," she said. "I'm gonna sneak into the computer lab so I can work on the documentary. It's due that Monday, and I'm guessing we'll have some last-minute edits to make."

"Right."

No. Not his moment.

Mr. Carrow buzzed in, sipping his coffee. He pointed at them like they were rock stars. "The power couple. How goes it?"

"Uh, good," Oliver said.

"How's life at the historical society? Find anything good?"

Ella opened her project binder and took out a folded piece of paper.

The folded piece of paper.

The love note.

"I found a love letter," she said.

Oliver thought his eardrums were exploding.

"Remember when I was rushing to transcribe that letter?" she asked Oliver. "The one Hal said we couldn't photocopy? My laptop died, so I had to do it by hand."

Oliver tried to answer but could only offer a dazed nod.

"Sounds juicy," Mr. Carrow said. He took the letter and read it. Oliver tried to sort out exactly what had happened and also get rid of the terrible feeling that he'd fallen backward over a cliff.

"What do you guys make of it?" Mr. Carrow asked.

"It matches his handwriting, I think," Ella said. "We couldn't copy the original, but I can double-check later this week."

Oliver hated roller coasters because of this feeling— that his guts had been pulled up into his diaphragm and then shoved down into his groin.

The letter had been written by *Stone?*

Not Ella.

"Ollie?" Mr. Carrow asked.

Get a grip, Ollie. Pull it together.

"The hard thing is," he said finally, "is that it's missing a location, date, and an address line."

Mr. Carrow stood on a chair and turned on the overhead projector. "And what do you think that means?"

"Maybe he wrote it but decided not to mail it to her," Ella said.

Ollie looked at her copy and scrambled for another not-idiotic thing to say. ". . . Or maybe he didn't plan on sending it because it wasn't a letter. Maybe it was a love note and he was going to actually give it to her."

"Now that's intriguing," Mr. Carrow said. "Why do you think that?"

Oliver skimmed the transcription until he got to the line he wanted. "He says that she's been by his side for a couple days, and that he's running out of time—that's why he decides to tell her. We know he died of dysentery at Gettysburg . . . so maybe it was for someone who took care of him. Like a nurse."

"Ollie—that's brilliant." Ella put her hand up for a high five, but because Oliver didn't give a lot of high fives he grabbed her hand instead and turned the whole thing into a really awkward midair handshake that was three seconds from turning into a game of Mercy.

Ian came into the room and gave them a weird look. Oliver let go of her hand.

"The theory is solid," Mr. Carrow said. "How can you test it?"

"Uh . . . I guess we could maybe check the muster rolls for his regiment. It might say where he died—like a field hospital or something. Maybe we can find a list of nurses who worked there? It's a super long shot, but maybe some of them left records we could check."

Ella nodded three times really fast. "Yes. That. We should do that."

"Agreed," Mr. Carrow said. He waved a finger between the two of them. "Quite a team you've made. I'm excited to see where it goes."

CHAPTER THIRTY

TENSION

"Muster rolls, muster rolls," Ella said as she logged into their Ancestry account. "Where do we find those?"

Oliver showed her how to find the collection and refine the search for the Pennsylvania 68th.

"They're scanned copies of the originals," he said as the pages loaded.

The document was like a giant spreadsheet listing Name, Rank, and so on. Oliver scanned with his finger down the name column until he found Stone.

> *Raymond Stone | Private | Enlisted Sept 62 | Died of dysentery, July 5 1863, Home of Charles Wentworth, Gettysburg.*

". . . Charles Wentworth," Oliver said. "That sounds really familiar."

"He died in somebody's house?" Ella asked. "Why not a hospital?"

"There were so many sick and wounded that most of the local homes and buildings became hospitals. Pretty much every civilian became a nurse or undertaker in the weeks after."

Ella slouched at that. "So it's going to be pretty much impossible to find out who Stone wrote the love note to."

Oliver blinked. "Not impossible." *Charles Wentworth . . . Charles Wentworth . . .* "Let me see something."

Oliver opened the massive document where they kept all the transcribed letters from the historical society. A quick search for "Wentworth" turned up the July 6 letter. "I knew I'd seen that name before: Susanna Wentworth. She's the lady who wrote Stone's last letter home after he died."

"Wait . . . wait . . ." Ella said, her eyes bouncing back and forth. "She took care of—she could have been his nurse. What if he wrote the note to *her*?"

Ella opened a new Ancestry window. In about ten minutes she'd narrowed the results down and found Susanna's info card. "She was Charles's daughter . . . about twenty years old when she took care of Stone. It could totally be her."

"Maybe . . . but a lot of women from different charity and church groups came to the town to help out. Other nurses could have taken care of him."

"He should have put her name on it," Ella said. "There wouldn't be so much confusion."

"You're telling me."

Ella slouched again. She seemed weirdly invested in figuring out what was up with the letter, which kind of made Oliver want to figure it out faster.

"Maybe we're thinking about this the wrong way," he said. "Gettysburg is a pretty historical place. The whole town is pretty much one big reenactment all year long. They have to have a historical society like ours. And if our town has records on Stone, then—"

"They might have something on the Wentworths," Ella said. "Ollie—that's brilliant. You're like . . . like a historical detective."

He loved that she said that. "This feels like a fist-pounding moment."

"Good instincts, but saying it takes some of the momentum away."

"Right."

He put his fist out, and she pounded it.

Ella found the historical society website for the Gettysburg area, but it didn't have many online sources, so they decided to call. After checking first with Mr.

Carrow, they went into the hall and slid to the floor, lockers against their backs.

"Adams County Historical Society," said an elderly woman after two rings. "Margaret Bolton speaking, how may I help you?"

"Hi, my name is Oliver Prichard. I'm a seventh grader doing a social studies project about a Union soldier from my town who died at Gettysburg. I was hoping you could help my partner and me track down some information about where he died, exactly."

"Oh, sounds interesting," Mrs. Bolton said. "We have a very extensive archive on civilian families before, during, and after the war. But we're not so up-to-date on technology; most of our documents remain in hard copy. I could put in a work order and hopefully get back to you by the end of the week? Who is it exactly that you're looking for?"

Oliver gave her Raymond Stone's name twice, spelling it each time to make sure there weren't any mistakes.

"And here's my cell phone and email," he said. He double-checked that she got those right too, thanked her, and then hung up.

They went back inside and started to pack up. Oliver was feeling pretty good about how class was ending, considering how horribly it had started.

"Who's Henry Weller?" Ella asked.

"Huh?"

Ella pointed to her screen. "Henry Weller. His Ancestry card is saved to our favorites board."

"H. Weller—the guy who wrote a couple letters to Stone's dad. I think he's the key to figuring out why Stone enlisted in the 68th. I'm pretty sure Weller paid him to fight in his place."

Oliver gave her the rundown of his research, ending with the email he sent to the Weller Group. "I was gonna tell you about it today but then, you know . . ." He indicated the love letter, still lying on top of Ella's binder.

"Sounds . . . complicated," Ella said.

Oliver thought she sounded a little icy. "I guess."

"So we should focus on things that were actually a part of his wartime experience."

"Like this love note."

"Exactly."

The rebellion churned in his gut again. "I don't think you understand what I might have found: an undocumented type of substitution for a lot of money. This could be totally new and undiscovered. A secret gold mine that Civil War historians don't even know about."

"A gold mine that only you know about."

"For right now, yeah."

"It's not important to the project."

Oliver stared at her for a few seconds. Was it possible to like someone and also want to tell her to back the heck off?

"It's definitely as important as him *not* playing baseball and *not* fighting and *maybe* writing some love note. And it might be important to the whole war and like, how soldiers actually fought."

They stared daggers at each other for a minute.

"Okay," she said, but it was another one of her *whatever* okays.

"Okay." He meant it as a *yeah, that's right whatever.*

"Just don't forget we have to proof Kevin's narrative and do the voiceovers this week." Ella logged off and packed her stuff up. "Oh—and we have to film your death."

-CHAPTER THIRTY-ONE-
DEATH BY DIARRHEA

Kevin read out loud from the dysentery page on WebMD. "It says your poop was, and I'm quoting here, *loose and filled with blood*." He turned to Oliver. "Got any fake blood?"

"Gross," Oliver said. He wondered if Stone was as embarrassed as he should have been about dying from something so stupid and disgusting.

"We can just put some red food dye in the dirty bed pan," Ella said. She readjusted the blankets on Oliver's bed and stood back to survey the scene. "Maybe sit up a little more."

Oliver scooted around. "Good?"

"Better. And we should probably get those out of the shot." Ella leaned over him to take a poster of General Ulysses S. Grant off the wall. She was exactly zero inches from him. Negative inches, actually. Her stomach was resting against his hip as she picked at the tape.

"What are you guys doing?"

"*Jeez,* Addie!" Oliver yelled. He'd sat up so quickly he was now basically burrowed in Ella's neck. "It's for the documentary. Now leave."

"Actually, I'm glad you're here," Ella said, finally unsticking the poster. "Could you get us some food dye? We're trying to make fake blood."

"To mix with our fake poop," Kevin added.

"Ewwwwww," Addie said, running up the steps.

"Careful with that," Oliver said as Ella laid the poster on the computer desk. His heart was still going a thousand miles an hour. Her neck smelled really good.

Ella sprinkled some water on his face to make it look like he was sweating. "Okay. Now act like you've been going to the bathroom nonstop for months and are about to die of stomach cramps and dehydration."

Oliver turned his head to the side and blinked lazily.

"You look like my uncle Donnie after he's hit the special punch at Christmas," Kevin said.

"Think of something sad," Ella suggested.

"Like what?"

"For me it's those orphan dog commercials with Sarah McLachlan," Kevin said. "You know, where they zoom in on puppies in cages and play 'I Will Remember You' in the background? Kills me. Every. Single. Time."

Oliver didn't have to think long to find a sad moment:

the exact second he realized Ella's love note was actually Stone's.

"That—right there," Ella said. "Hold that face."

Addie stomped back down with a tiny bottle of red food dye.

"This is about to get awesomely gory," Kevin said.

"Thanks, Addie," Ella said.

"Can I watch?"

"Sure. You could be like our assistant. Get us things we need."

"Like snacks," Kevin said. "I recall a discussion about Capri Suns—specifically a variety pack."

"Mom says you guys drank all the Capri Suns, so we're out until the next Costco run," Addie said.

"Budget cuts. Happens to all the great projects near the end."

"Ollie, time to die," Ella said.

Ten minutes later Oliver's stomach and back felt like they'd been through a trash compactor from all the fake cramping and writhing. Who knew pretending to die would make him feel like he was actually going to die.

"Is that good?" he panted.

Ella reviewed the footage on her phone. "Good. Now for the climax: the actual moment of your death. It needs to be really dramatic."

"I consulted with the Head Writing Consultant," Kevin said. "And he agrees you need to sell it."

Oliver closed his eyes. He hunched forward and let out some of the worst groans he could conjure. He convulsed like there was an earthquake in his lower intestine. He balled up the blankets in his fists. He clawed at his gut. He took in a great, mighty breath of air.

And then he collapsed.

"That," Kevin said, "was disturbingly amazing."

"So you didn't die of getting shot?" Addie asked from her perch on the couch arm.

Oliver was still out of breath. "No. I got dysentery."

"What's that?"

"It's a bacterial infection of your intestines," Kevin said. "You poop blood and usually die of dehydration."

"But you're a soldier," Addie said. "Soldiers die in battle."

"Most soldiers actually died of disease," Ella said. "And tons of those died of dysentery like the guy Oliver is playing."

Addie went over to Oliver's desk drawer and took out a Time-Life Civil War book. "The guys on this cover are fighting." She grabbed another one. "Here too. And here—"

"We get it, Addie," Oliver said.

Addie sat back down. "It's just funny. Ollie got a

soldier who died from disease, when he spends every Saturday pretending to fight—"

"It's not *funny*, Addie. It's *stupid*. So just shut up about it."

As soon as the words were out of his mouth, Oliver knew he'd made a Big Mistake.

The newly hired assistant ran upstairs. Oliver heard her crying for his mom.

Great.

The silence was deafening. Oliver looked at Kevin and Ella.

Kevin tiptoed to the computer desk and pretended to be typing; Ella packed up her tripod. Neither of them would look at him.

"Guys." Oliver threw back the covers and stretched his legs out. "I didn't mean that. I'm sorry. She's just really good at annoying me."

Awkward silence.

"I'm sorry," he said. "It's just—"

"Dude," Kevin said. "Don't make it worse."

Oliver felt like his lungs were overinflated. It wasn't healthy to hold it in any longer on this issue. He just had to say it.

"No matter how cool we make this project, you're never going to convince me that Private Stone is—"

"Who wants to stay for tacos?" Oliver's mom shouted from the top of the steps.

More awkward silence.

"Everyone alive down there?"

"Hard or soft shell, Mrs. P?" Kevin asked.

"Both."

"You convinced me. I'm in."

"Great. Ella, are you staying?"

Ella waited a few seconds. "Okay. Let me text my mom."

"Why don't you text up here? We know how bad the service is down there."

Ella grinned a little as the tension broke.

Oliver did too, but lost the smile when Ella threw him a stare.

"I'm gonna wash my hands," Kevin said, heading to the bathroom.

"It's not stupid, you know," Ella said as the door clicked shut.

Oliver shuffled around on the bed. "I know."

"Everyone's life matters, no matter how they died."

"I know."

"Stop saying you know." Her words had a jagged edge to them. "And start acting like it."

CHAPTER THIRTY-TWO

THE COOLEST TEACHER YOU NEVER KNEW

"Make room at your tables for Mrs. Mason's students," Mr. Carrow said as his classroom overfilled. "Today is gonna be a little different."

"No kidding," Kevin said to Oliver, sitting down next to him. "Scoot. I'm majorly cramped here."

"Can't," Oliver said, with a quick glance at Ella.

"I can see there's room," Kevin said.

Oliver bumped into Ella as he scooted. "Sorry."

No response. Things were still a little icy post-death-by-dysentery incident.

"So how come your class is even here?" Oliver asked.

"Some sort of combined English–social studies thing on slavery—stations and stuff. Kids in second period said Mr. Carrow cried."

"What?"

"Just what I heard."

Some of Mrs. Mason's students carried in the old-school wooden lectern she taught from and set it next to the projector screen. She and Mr. Carrow whispered to each other, then Mr. Carrow stood up and waved his hands wildly for everyone to quiet down.

"Good to have you, Mrs. Mason's students. A little tight, yeah, but we'll make do. Ian, hit the lights."

The room went dark and an image came into focus on the screen: a drawing of an African American man on one knee, his chained hands raised like he was praying. The text above him read *Am I Not a Man and Brother?*

"Before this unit we talked about slavery— origins, the slave trade, an enslaved person's experience, and how it divided the nation and caused the Civil War. But what about the impact that slaves had on the war effort, like when they slowed their work or ran away to Union lines? And what about free African Americans in the North? Did they join the Union Army? Did they fight in battles? These are important questions we're gonna think about today as we continue to examine the war from all angles."

Oliver snuck a glance at Mrs. Mason. He couldn't help it. He wondered if talking about slavery made her feel awkward. It would make Oliver feel awkward if he was the only black person with a bunch of white people and he had to talk about slavery. Then again, maybe she was used to it. She'd been working here since pretty much the dawn of time.

Mrs. Mason caught his eye. Oliver froze. He waited for her to bore holes into his soul.

She smiled.

Yeah—this day was bonkers.

"We're going to rotate through a couple stations that explore the African American experience during the war," Mr. Carrow said. "But first a very special guest is going to share a very personal story. You know her already, but let's give her a nice welcome: the one and only Mrs. Mason."

At first nobody clapped, but Mr. Carrow really hammed it up, so everyone joined in.

"That's too kind of you, Mr. Carrow," Mrs. Mason said. She cleared her throat. She fiddled with her notes on the podium like she'd forgotten what she was going to say. The silence dragged.

Finally, Mrs. Mason fingered a silver locket hanging around her neck and took a breath. "Social studies is not my area of expertise, not exactly. But I am part of a story that has its roots in the Civil War. Today I'd like to share that story with you."

Mr. Carrow moved the PowerPoint slide ahead to a newspaper ad with big block lettering.

TO COLORED MEN
54TH REGIMENT!
Massachusetts Volunteers,
African Descent!
$100 Bounty!
At the expiration of the terms of service
Pay of $13 a Month!
And State Aid to Families.
Recruiting Office,
Cor. Cambridge & North Russell Sts. Boston

"On January 1, 1863, Abraham Lincoln issued the Emancipation Proclamation," Mrs. Mason said. "Mr. Carrow has told you how this freed slaves in the Confederate states; but it also called for the enrollment of black soldiers into the Union Army and Navy. The Governor of Massachusetts, John Andrew, began recruiting black troops from all parts of the Union to form the 54th Massachusetts Regiment using broadside posters like the one pictured here. And it was probably a poster like this that my great-great-grandfather saw while he was working on the loading docks in Philadelphia."

Oliver heard it happen—the air left the room as everybody sucked in breath.

Mrs. Mason was descended from a *Civil War soldier*?

"No way," Oliver whispered.

Mr. Carrow moved to the next slide: an image of an African American soldier in full uniform, sitting for a photograph in front of a canvas painted with hills and trees. Oliver thought he looked calm and happy— hands folded in his lap, tiny smile on his face, cap a little crooked. Proud.

"Linus was born a slave on a small Maryland farm around 1845, we think," Mrs. Mason said. "I can't be certain, as he communicated this story orally to his children, who then wrote it down for their children— including my grandfather." She rubbed the silver locket again. "He escaped as a teenager, before the war, and made his way to Philadelphia, where he got a job in the shipyards."

"Her ancestor was a Civil War soldier *and* a runaway slave?" Oliver whispered.

"Mrs. Mason is officially the coolest teacher I never really knew," Kevin murmured.

"Linus went up to Boston to join the 54th and survived the battles you'll read about during your station activity today. He returned to Philadelphia after the war, got his old job back, met a girl at church, and a century and a half later, here I am."

She smiled at that little joke, but got serious real quick.

"I think fighting in this war meant something different to black troops. It's important for us to understand that. The Confederacy threatened to execute them if they were captured in battle, or worse, to sell them back into slavery. Men like Linus were risking something different from the white troops they were fighting alongside—they were risking their freedom to fight for a great liberation. And they were picking up a fight that had been started by their ancestors, who found pockets of happiness in the midst of bondage, or took part in work slowdowns, or ran away. These black soldiers were willing to lay down their lives alongside their white countrymen to prove that they *were* their countrymen."

She lifted the silver locket off her chest and opened it.

"Linus bought a small portrait of himself in uniform and tucked it inside this locket as a birthday present to his wife. She passed it on to her daughter-in-law, and it made it all the way to me. I keep it to remember what he and other black soldiers were willing to sacrifice so that I might live free."

She stopped. Oliver looked up at her. She looked different, softer. He felt proud and sad at the same time.

Kevin nudged him and pointed to Mr. Carrow. He was lost in something too, Oliver saw. More serious and solemn than a monk. Like he was underneath some heavy burden he wasn't used to.

"How 'bout a round of applause for Mrs. Mason," Mr. Carrow said. Students clapped, but softly. Oliver felt it too: This wasn't really a celebrating sort of occasion. "Ian, lights please. I'm gonna pass out some folders with your table's topic. I want you to dive into the reading and answer the questions at the end. Watch the timer on the screen so you know how much time is left in each station. Got it? Good."

"That," Kevin said, "was intense. Holy crap. My heart is pounding. Feel my heart." He grabbed Oliver's hand and put it on his chest. "Boom boom boom."

"It's pretty crazy," Oliver said. "Really intense and really cool. Kind of the opposite of our guy."

Ella shoved a reading in Oliver's direction.

"Until we figure out this very cool love letter connection," Oliver finished.

Kevin shook his head.

Oliver was really striking out here.

"Number one," Kevin said. *"In your own words, describe the 1863 Draft Riots of New York City."*

"A bunch of angry Irish people were mad that Lincoln was forcing them to enlist in the Union Army to fight a war that would bring even more African Americans north to take their jobs," Oliver said. "They burned a bunch of buildings and started attacking people."

"Nailed it."

"You didn't even look at the reading," Ella said.

"Didn't have to," Oliver said. "I brushed up on the draft when I was finding H. Weller."

"H. who now?" Kevin asked.

Oliver gave Kevin the lowdown. Ella rolled her eyes at least twice.

"That," Kevin said, "is super cool. Continue exploring."

"We have less than a week left," Ella said. "We don't have time for that kind of distraction."

"We're just waiting around for Mrs. Bolton to call us," Oliver said. "And I already told you, it might be a whole new discovery about the war."

"And I told you that you're getting lost in a bunch of details that don't matter instead of our actual project."

The rebellion launched from his gut up to his throat. "And I'm telling you that you're being kind of a—"

"Whoa whoa whoa," Kevin cut in. "Let's take this down a notch. We're all a little emotional right now; I blame that on Mrs. Mason's epic past. What we need to do is compromise."

"I've been doing a lot for her whole love letter thing," Oliver said. His throat felt tight and the words flew out like bullets. He wasn't just mad; he felt a little hurt. "I think it's time she gave in a little."

"Ella, the man has a point," Kevin said.

She scanned Oliver's face and looked away. "You're right. I'm sorry." Her voice was smaller all of a sudden. "I just really want to find the person Stone wrote this love letter to."

A minute ago he wanted to scream at her; now he wanted to hug her.

How was this possible?

Who knew these things.

CHAPTER THIRTY-THREE

THE REPLY

To: privateoliverprichard@gmail.com
Subject: Henry Weller

Dear Oliver,

A customer service representative forwarded me your email regarding our company's president during the late 1800s and early 1900s, Henry Weller. I shared it with Mr. Eugene Weller, our current bank president and great-great-grandson of Henry Weller, who found it very interesting. While I can't promise a response before your project is due, I will be in touch with any information.

Good luck.
Sincerely,
Amanda DeFrancesca
Senior Assistant
The Weller Group

CHAPTER THIRTY-FOUR

THE SOCIETY OF PEOPLE WHO THINK WAR IS BAD

Oliver reread the email probably as many times as he'd read Ella's/Stone's love note. Was that weird—that a potential historical discovery made him as excited as a potential girlfriend?

Maybe. Probably.

Who knew these things.

Not that it really mattered. Without the love note, and considering her almost constant annoyance at his little side project, Ella's Scorecard of Emotions was looking pretty disappointing.

In the basement, Oliver turned on his computer and pulled up his research.

Theory #3: Stone enlisted in the 68th as a substitute for some guy named H. Weller.

How to prove:

- Find more letters from H. Weller
  - Find out who H. Weller was
    - ~~Google the crap out of him~~
    - Search on Ancestry.com
      - Weller Bank president was also named Henry Weller (says so on their website)
      - Society of Friends?
      - Find out if this is the same H. Weller who wrote Stone's dad those letters (emailed)

Oliver stared at the phrase *Society of Friends* for a while and then started googling the term.

- Society of Friends
  - Also called Quakers
  - Christian group
  - Started 1650
  - Big on "inner light"?
  - Big on peace
  - Hate war

Oliver knew there were a ton of Quakers in Philly—the whole state of Pennsylvania had been founded by a Quaker, William Penn. But what did that have to do with Stone? Oliver stared at his notes and the letters H.

Weller had written to Stone's dad. He felt like a detective. The answer had to be here somewhere.

He called Kevin to talk about it out loud, like Mr. Daniels said real detectives do.

No answer.

Oliver hovered over Ella's name for a second. No way she'd want to talk about this.

"I'd talk to you about it," he told Stone, "but I really need an actual person this time. No offense."

He went up to the living room to find his parents, but they seemed pretty into one of those police shows.

Okay, time for the last resort. Oliver went up to Addie's room and listened to her do scales on the electric keyboard before he walked in.

"Hey."

"You're not allowed in my room," she said. "No boys are allowed in my room, ever. Dad said so."

"He didn't mean me."

"You're a boy."

"I need to talk out a problem with you."

"Why?"

"Because that's what you're supposed to do when you have a problem."

"Is this about your girlfriend?"

"I don't have a girlfriend."

"Ella."

"I don't have a girlfriend."

"Can I keep playing while you talk?"

"Uh, sure. Just turn down the volume."

Oliver sketched out everything he'd learned so far about Stone, H. Weller, and the Quakers in about ten minutes. He felt like he was getting somewhere by just rehashing the details over and over—like those old gold miners who would sift through river mud looking for nuggets.

"That's a good name," Addie said. "The Society of Friends."

"Uh-huh." He didn't even think she'd been listening. "Wait—what do you mean?"

"They want everybody in the world to be friends with each other, and friends don't fight."

"Sometimes they do," Oliver said. "You fight with your friends."

"Not argue—fight with weapons."

"Yeah. They hated war."

"We need people like that now."

"Uh-huh."

"We should all be friends. War is bad."

Oliver decided that Addie had reached the end of her usefulness. "Okay. Thanks."

He put one foot in the hall, then stopped.

He turned back to his sister. "War is bad."

"I just said that."

". . . But what if you thought this war wasn't?"

"What war? Iraq?"

"No, the Civil War," Oliver said. "What if you thought the war was good? Not like *good*, but . . . important. What if you thought it was *really* important, and you wanted to fight, but you couldn't because it was against your religion. What would you do?"

"War is bad," Addie said.

For a second Oliver lost his train of thought. "But Weller could've hired anyone to fight for him . . . why Stone? How did they even know each other . . . ?"

"I need to practice," Addie said.

And then he had it.

Oliver ran over to his sister and hugged her hard.

"Dad said this is why boys aren't allowed in my room. You're a distraction," Addie said.

Oliver raced downstairs to his computer.

> To: adefrancesca@wellergroup.org
> Subject: Re: Henry Weller
>
>
> Dear Amanda DeFrancesca,
>
>
> This is Oliver again. I'm not trying to bother you or anything, but I was wondering if your company had

any archives from the 1850s and 1860s? If you do, could you search and see if a Raymond Stone or any Stone was maybe a customer of the bank?

I know you're already looking for the contract thing, so I really appreciate it. I know you're really busy, but I just wanted to remind you that my project is due in six days.

Thanks and sorry for bothering you again.
From Oliver

CHAPTER THIRTY-FIVE

PRIVATE STONE'S DEATHBED CRUSH

"Three days and she hasn't emailed me back," Oliver said.

Kevin just barely finished chewing a meatball. "Rich people are always really busy. Like my aunt Mindy. She drives a Porsche and lives ten minutes away but always tells my mom she's too busy to hang out."

"I guess it's too late now anyway," Oliver said. "Ella will be happy, at least."

"Would have been pretty cool if it all connected somehow."

"Uh-huh."

Oliver stared at the line of people outside the cafeteria waiting to buy tickets for the spring dance. It must have been twenty kids deep.

"Are you going to the dance?" he asked Kevin.

"Of course."

"What?"

"What?

"Uh, nothing," Oliver said. "I'm just surprised."

"That I have a date."

"No . . . just surprised that you'd want to go."

"I don't, really. But Cindy does."

"Who's Cindy?"

"The sixth grader I was telling you about. Artsy. Too busy being awesome to worry about being on the Honor Roll. Can sometimes be seen interpretive dancing during choir? I asked her yesterday."

"Huh."

"Aren't you going?"

"No."

"I thought you'd ask Ella."

Oliver felt like he was falling again. "I don't know."

"'Cause you're terrified if you ask, she'll serve up a steaming hot plate of rejection?"

"Pretty much." Oliver spotted Ella outside, at her old table—the one she *used* to sit at before they were friends. Her earbuds were in, and he could guess what she was reading. "She's already going by herself, anyway. She said her sister is making her, and she's just going to sneak into the computer lab and work on any last-minute edits to the documentary."

"Ella is going to wear a dress?"

"I know. It doesn't make sense."

He snapped a finger and pointed at Oliver. "You should just show up. Be like, 'Oh—what are you doing here?' Like a sneak attack date. And then just hang with her the rest of the time in the lab."

"Isn't that a little . . . stalkerish?"

"There's a fine line between stalkerish and romantic," Kevin said, "but I think you're within the law here."

"It's the actual dancing part too. Not exactly my thing."

"These dances are like gym class with dresses and ties. Nobody dances with people they like. They just find their friends and play on their phones."

Oliver's pocket vibrated and he reached for his phone. The number was from an area code he didn't recognize, and he almost let it go to voicemail when—

Amanda DeFrancesca?

Could she be calling him with H. Weller answers?

"Hello?" he said loudly into the phone. It was almost cleanup time and the cafeteria was turning into a zoo.

"Oliver—this—Bolton—Adams County—"

His heart sank. Then he remembered he hadn't given Amanda his cell phone number.

Duh.

"Hold on," he yelled into the phone.

Weaving through tables, Oliver headed for the outdoor patio to flag down Ella.

"It's Mrs. Bolton—from the historical society," he said, pointing to the phone.

Ella ripped out her earbuds. "What?"

"Margaret—Bolton—from the—"

"Oliver? Can you hear me now?" Mrs. Bolton asked.

"Yes, yes—sorry, Mrs. Bolton. It's lunchtime here and it's really loud."

"Oh, that's okay. Would you like me to call back—?"

"No no, it's fine. Now is good." He mouthed "Archive" to Ella, and her eyes suddenly sparkled. She herded him over to the wrought iron fence near the parking lot where it was quieter and took the phone from him to put it on speaker.

"Hi, Mrs. Bolton, Ella here," she said.

"Oh, hello dear. Good good. I wanted to let you know I did some digging about the Gettysburg resident you asked about—Susanna Wentworth. Took me a little longer than I thought, but I think I've uncovered some papers that will be very helpful to your project."

"That's awesome," Ella said. She beamed at Oliver. "What did you find?"

"Boxes," she said. "Three boxes, to be exact, of letters, diaries, business and estate papers—all donated to us by the Wentworth family."

Ella grabbed Oliver's shoulder and shook it violently. It felt like the tendons were doused in lighter fluid and set on fire, but he didn't care. Seeing her this happy was amazing—even if he had no idea why she was so invested in this.

"Mrs. Bolton, this is exactly what we've been looking for," Ella said. "Is there a username or password we need to get on your website and access it?"

"Oh, I'm afraid none of these have been digitized. You'd have to come here in person to examine them."

Ella's smile went slack. "Oh."

"I'm sorry. But you are more than welcome to visit the archive and go through everything for as long as you want."

Oliver could see the cafeteria had almost emptied completely. Time to wrap this up.

"Okay," he said because Ella wasn't saying anything. "Thanks again for all your help."

"Certainly, dear," she said, and hung up.

"Sorry," Oliver said, and he was. Not that the love note thing didn't work out, but because she was so sad.

Ella gave him a serious look. "What's the absentee policy for the 104th Pennsylvania Volunteers?"

"Uh, why?"

"Because we're going on a road trip this weekend." She dialed a number on her phone. "My mom probably has a house showing on Saturday, but I'll ask my dad to drive us." Her dad picked up. "Dad, it's me. Yeah, no—everything's fine. Listen: I need a ride to Gettysburg this weekend, for my social studies project. We found—"

She stopped, clearly cut off. Her face grew harder by the second.

"Fine. Uh-huh. Whatever. Okay. Bye." She stabbed the screen with her thumb to end the call.

"He's busy?"

"Shocker."

"Sorry."

"Wait." Her fingers flew over the phone as she constructed a text. "My sister's been saying she wants to hang out more this summer, and I did let her take me dress shopping. Maybe—"

Ella stopped short. She showed him the reply.

Going to the beach with Kara. Ask Dad.

"That sucks," Oliver said.

Ella shoved her phone into her pocket and stared at the parking lot.

And then she said something incredibly strange.

"I am the Private Stone of my own life."

Oliver had no idea what that meant. But he knew exactly what to say.

"I'll ask my parents if they can drive."

"Really?"

"Friends don't let friends not go to Gettysburg to find historical documents," he said.

Ella threw her arms around his neck. "Ollie: You're amazing."

CHAPTER THIRTY-SIX

THE ROAD TRIP

"That's a tough one," Kevin said. He dragged a box of Capri Suns across Oliver's kitchen counter and started shoving them into his backpack. "How did she say it? Was it like 'You're aMAZing!' or 'YOU'RE AMAZING!'"

Oliver watched his soggy cereal floating around the bowl. "The first one. I think."

"Did she hug you before or after she said it?"

Oliver replayed the moment in his head, a thousand butterflies slamming around in his gut. He'd told Kevin about the hug—and the Scorecard of Emotions—to get some clarity. "During. Or maybe a little before."

"Okay. On one hand, a friend might say that, because what you did was pretty amazing. The hugging is tricky, but some people just hug when they get excited. Take Cindy for example: She hugs me every time I see her between classes. Between you and me, that girl is getting pretty clingy."

"That's very helpful."

"Tell you what: I'll be your wingman in Gettysburg today—be on the lookout for stuff in the 'More than Friends' category. That's a mouthful—let's call it MTF. Deal?"

"Thanks.

"Friends don't let friends miss obvious signals to clarify if their special someone also has a crush on them. You can have that life phrase, if you want." Kevin counted the Capri Suns in his bag and then added one more for good measure. "Your romantic issues aside, you gotta admit that finding something about this Susanna person in Gettysburg would make our documentary beyond epic. The only thing better than a tragedy is a tragic romance, and we might have fallen into one."

Oliver's mom whisked into the kitchen. "Ella's mom just pulled up. Ready?"

"Ready, Mrs. P," Kevin said. "And thanks again for nixing my mom's neon-orange shirt plan. I'd rather get lost than be found wearing that thing."

"What are you gonna do while we're at the historical society?" Oliver asked his mom.

"Your dad wants to see a couple of the museums. Maybe part of the battlefield if we have time."

"Can't you wait until we're done?"

"Hmm, probably not. Ella's mom said she has to be back home for the dance."

The injustice of it almost shoved him off the stool. *He* should be reliving the greatest Civil War moments on the battlefield, not his parents.

Oliver's dad came in from the garage with Addie trailing behind. "The USS *Prichard* is prepared for departure."

"Mr. P, I would like to volunteer as assistant navigator," Kevin said as they filed into the garage. "I was in the Boy Scouts for half a year. Why I left isn't important. Okay fine, there was an incident during a camping trip with a raccoon I'd rather not get into right now, but the point is that I've got really good spatial awareness."

"How about an iPhone?" Oliver's dad asked. Kevin held his up. "Great. Plug in the address and let me know if I make a wrong turn."

Oliver watched Ella bouncing on her heels by the van. Today's tank top was aqua. Kind of like her eyes.

"Ella!" Addie screamed. She ran up and gave her a high five.

"Got something for you." Ella pulled out her phone and one of those car connector cables. "I found this band on YouTube who turns classical music into hard rock ballads. I was listening to it last night and heard a very familiar song . . ." She hummed the opening to Andante.

"That's *awesome*," Addie squealed.

"I should really be near the cockpit," Kevin said, plopping into a captain's chair.

Addie claimed the other. "I get carsick back there."

Which put Ella next to Oliver in the back row. She smelled like strawberry shortcake.

"Ollie, this was really awesome of you," she said. "I'm sorry you had to miss drill."

"It's okay. This way I can't almost stab myself with my own bayonet."

She fist-pounded him, but this time her hand opened after their knuckles hit. She made an explosion sound.

"What's that?" he asked.

"Blowing it up. It's only for super-amazing special occasions. Like this."

He gulped. "Cool."

MTF bro, Kevin texted. *MTF.*

The hard rock version of Andante got old before they'd even pulled onto the freeway.

"Again," Addie demanded.

"I think that's enough for now," Oliver's mom said. She unplugged Ella's phone to pass it back to her, but Ella handed it back to Addie. She dug through her pocket and pulled out some earbuds for Addie. Her worn pack of cards fell out too.

Addie shoved the earbuds in and started head banging. Ella took the cards out and fanned them toward Oliver. "Working on a new trick. Pick one."

He did. Ace of hearts. "Okay."

She arranged the cards back into a smooth pile. "Now put it on top." He set it on top of the stack, and she placed her palm over it. "Hit it."

"What?"

"Slap the deck."

"Uh. Okay." He slapped the deck.

"Harder. Hard enough to knock the top card to another spot."

"That's not possible."

"Ollie, just slap it."

So he did.

Ella ran her index finger along the top card and then flipped it over.

Eight of spades.

"What—"

"You slapped it pretty hard."

"Where's my card?" Oliver asked.

Ella grinned. She flipped it back over, but must have fumbled something, because it looked like two cards this time. She held up his ace of hearts. "You flip two at a time. If you do it right, it's impossible to tell."

"That's pretty awesome."

"Still working on it."

"According to Google Maps we should arrive at ten fifty-eight," Kevin announced. "Now, if we go five over the speed limit—which my dad says cops don't care about—we can shave off ten minutes."

Oliver's dad adjusted the rearview mirror. "Aye-aye, Captain."

"Someone named Charlie texted you," Addie told Ella. "Is Charlie your boyfriend?"

Air raced out of Oliver's lungs.

"Who's Charlie?" he asked.

Ella leaned forward and looked at the text. "My sister."

"Oh. Right." Instant relief.

The phone buzzed again. Addie read the next text aloud. "Charlie says, *Don't come home without asking him.*"

"Addie—"

"Charlie says, *You don't want to go to your first dance alone, so you better just woman up and—*"

Ella almost strangled Addie with the earbuds as she grappled for her phone. Her face was bright red. "Here—I'll just keep it for now. You can listen more on the way home."

Addie fake-pouted.

Oliver's stomach knotted.

Was that text about *him?*

His phone buzzed.

It was about you, Kevin texted. *MTFMTFMTF.*

Ella and Oliver both stared straight ahead. Soon the van was twisting around back roads with the windows down, and the tension had loosened just enough for Oliver to text the question bouncing around in his gut.

Ask who what?

Nothing, Ella texted back. *My sister is just nosy.*

Nosy about what?

Ella took in a giant breath. *She wants me to ask you to come to the dance with me tonight.*

Oliver thought he was floating. *As your date?*

Yeah.

But you don't even want to go to the dance.

I know.

You said you were just going to work on the project.

I am. But I can't tell her that.

I still don't get why you're even going.

It's complicated.

Oliver stared out the window at a cow. He wondered if the cow ever had a crush on another cow, but was having so much trouble reading her signals that he wasn't sure when or if to make a move.

The cow lifted its tail and took a dump.

Tell Charlie you asked me and I said yes, Oliver typed. *I'll go with you.*

The terrible ". . ." when someone is typing a message appeared. It always felt like it was there forever. Oliver could see her fingers flying, but then deleting the words.

Maybe he'd gotten her side of the scorecard totally wrong.

Maybe she didn't even have a "More Than Friends" category for him on her Scorecard of Emotions. After all, he'd written hers.

The . . . was making him crazy. He had to walk it back. *We can just walk in together and then we'll go work on the project,* he wrote.

. . .

OK, said her message when it finally arrived. *Thanks. Sure.*

Oliver had a flash-forward of him and Ella sitting in the lab. Alone. She'd be in her dress, looking like weekend Ella times twenty. He'd probably look like a stuffed sausage in the suit he'd worn for Easter last year.

But it would be just the two of them.

On a date.

Kind of.

Sorry again that you had to miss drill, Ella typed. *Totally worth it.*

★ ★ ★

"My mom says the only time it's not embarrassing to eat at Wendy's is when you're on a road trip," Kevin said.

Ella peered at the giant drive-through menu. "We never get fast food. My mom says it's not part of our health plan."

"Well, yeah," Kevin said. "That's the point. It's horrible for you, but it tastes like heaven."

Oliver watched the cars zipping by on the turnpike out his left window as the van inched forward in the line. Going from back roads to the highway had apparently made Addie carsick, so Oliver's dad decided to stop and get her some ginger ale.

"I read on the Internet that Wendy's makes a burger they don't put on the menu," Kevin said. "It's like the Holy Grail of burgers."

Ella leaned forward. "What makes it so special?"

"It's four patties of meat. It's called 'the meat cube.'"

"The meat cube," she whispered. Ella dug into her pocket and produced two twenty-dollar bills. "Is anyone else hungry?"

"It's not even ten o'clock," Oliver said. "I'm pretty sure they don't make burgers this early."

"Let's find out," Ella said. "Mr. and Mrs. P: My mom gave me some money for the trip, and I'd love to buy breakfast for everyone. Or a meat cube for anyone who wants to try it."

"I won't turn down sausage at this hour," Oliver's dad said.

"That's very kind of you, Ella," said his mom.

"One milkshake, please," Addie said.

Oliver gave her a look. "I thought your stomach hurt."

"I'm feeling better."

Ten minutes later the van was back on the highway smelling like a Wendy's kitchen.

"Ohhhhhh," Kevin groaned. He grabbed his stomach and leaned forward. "The meat cube. It's having its way with me."

"*That*," Ella exclaimed, "was exactly as good as I'd hoped." She wiped her mouth and crumpled the wrapper. "My parents don't know what they're missing." She gave Oliver's home fries a *you gonna finish those?* look.

He gave her the rest. He was too nervous/excited to eat anyway.

Because he was going to the dance.

Kind of.

With Ella.

A girl who could eat four patties of meat in ten minutes.

CHAPTER THIRTY-SEVEN

LITTLE SOLDIER, BIG WAR

Ella checked the picture on her phone. "This is it."

Oliver squinted at the house set twenty yards off the street: faded white siding, two giant brick chimneys sticking into the sky, probably twelve tiny gabled windows, and a screened-in porch

"I guess all historical societies look like old people's houses," he said.

"Prime selfie spot located." Kevin ran over to a maroon sign ten feet away that read ADAMS COUNTY HISTORICAL SOCIETY: THE BATTLE OF GETTYSBURG RESEARCH CENTER.

They took a quick picture, and then Oliver got his book bag from the trunk. "I'll call you when we're done," he said to his dad.

"Did you get your sandwiches?" his mom asked.

"Got 'em."

"Okay, have fun!" She waved and they drove off to the battlefield. Oliver almost chased after them.

Ella led them up an old brick stairway and along the winding entry walkway that took them around to the front of the house.

A faraway voice called, "Good morning!"

Oliver looked up and saw an older woman with gray hair waving from a second-story window.

"Mrs. Bolton?" Ella called up.

"That's me. You must be Ella. And you two are . . ." She trailed off, looking from Oliver to Kevin.

"Kevin—Head Writing Consultant," Kevin announced. "My extreme pleasure to make your acquaintance. Nice house."

Oliver gave a half wave. "Hi. I'm Oliver."

"I'll come down and let you inside."

A minute later, a side door creaked open and the short and stocky Margaret Bolton invited them into a small entryway. She had on a plain dress that looked a little Amish and wore those big white sneakers that old people wear. Oliver wondered if Mrs. Bolton was the old person who lived in this house. It would make sense.

"I'm so pleased you made the trip," Mrs. Bolton said, smiling so her face crinkled up. "Impressed, actually. Never had middle school students in here to do serious historical work. Mostly just grad students and authors."

"Thanks for having us," Ella said. "It's very kind of you to let us examine these papers."

"You're doing us a favor too. We only have a limited staff, so we can't transcribe *every* document."

She led them through the entryway to a small desk with a sign that read ABSOLUTELY NO CAMERAS ALLOWED. "Just need you to sign in first—standard procedure." When they'd all written their names, Mrs. Bolton walked them into the reading room. A big oak table sat in the middle with some chairs, and a few computer stations were set off in the corner. Like the historical society in their town, bookshelves covered every inch of wall space.

"I've pulled the Wentworth items already," Mrs. Bolton said. She gestured to the three office boxes that sat on the big oak table. "Here they are."

Ella eyed them like they were meat cubes. "Wow."

"Now, you have to be very careful when examining these items." Mrs. Bolton pulled three pairs of white cotton gloves from a cabinet. "The documents are in good shape because we keep them in a climate-controlled setting, and we ask all researchers to wear gloves when touching them."

"Keeps the oil on our hands from speeding up the decay," Ella said. "The guy who runs our historical society showed us."

"Oh, very good then. I'll be in my office two flights up—just give a holler if you need anything."

Ella threw her stuff into a chair and pulled on a pair of gloves. "Will do. Thanks again, Mrs. Bolton."

"Happy hunting," she said, heading up the switchback steps.

Ella leaned on the table for a few seconds. "Let's do this."

She lifted the top off the first box and stared inside.

Kevin peeked into the second box and wrinkled his nose. "Smells like a document coffin."

Ella lifted out several stacks of paper encased in plastic and read the labels. "Estate papers." Something caught her eye and her face lit up. She took out a gaudy bronze picture frame that held a sepia-toned portrait of four people. The girl, who looked about Ella's age in the picture, sat beside her mom while her dad stood behind them. A toddler sat on the ground and stared the other way.

"Hi, Susanna," she said.

"How come they're not smiling?" Kevin asked.

"Nobody smiled back then," Oliver said. He took the top off his box and glanced down at the stacks of paper. "They treated all photographs like very serious school pictures. All very proper and stuff."

Ella peered into his box and almost shoved him aside. "Ollie—look."

He followed her finger to several small, leather-bound books stacked along the bottom of the box. Oliver counted twelve. "Diaries."

Ella opened each cover to check the dates.

"Bingo," she whispered. "Susanna's diary from 1861 to 1863." She set it flat on the table and carefully leafed through the pages. *"July 3, 1863. Cannon fire can be heard all day as if right outside our door*—Ollie, start typing. *Father says war is a plague that destroys the land. Thank heaven Thomas and Solomon are far from this place."*

"Must be her brothers or something," Oliver said, opening the laptop.

"Or her other boyfriends," Kevin said.

Ella ignored him and kept reading. *"July 4. This Independence Day is marked by sorrow instead of celebration. We have set up sickbeds for the wounded. Near twenty have arrived with grave injuries. I fetch water and empty bedpans. One soldier coughs constantly and is very weak. His name is Raymond. Mother fears he may perish. He is kind to me and speaks often of his home.*

"July 5. Raymond's flux has worsened. Mother fears

he will go home to our Lord soon. He has grown too weak to hold a pen. I promised to write his parents should he pass. We spoke late into the night and I feared each sentence would be our last."

Ella's voice wobbled. Hearing her made Oliver's throat tighten.

"July 6. More soldiers arrived today but I cannot care. Raymond has died. I woke this morning and found him in that final slumber. I cried terribly. I will write his family and send his belongings, save the picture he gave me. I have set it on my nightstand. I pray for his family."

Oliver looked up from the screen and saw a wet streak down the side of Ella's face. He had no idea *why* she was crying, but he really wanted to hug her.

Ella set the open diary on the table and—as if they'd willed it—a small bit of paper fell out.

Kevin picked up the photograph. "He's uglier than I thought he'd be," he said. "I mean not *ugly,* but you know. Scruffy, I guess."

Oliver sized him up: not really tall, kinda broad. Solid. Brown hair and a short beard. One thing no one could deny: He looked awesome in his Union uniform.

Ella turned the photograph over. *Pvt. R. Stone* was scrawled in cursive.

"And there it is," Oliver said. He shut the laptop

and raced to pack up. "We can probably see part of the battlefield before we go home."

Ella sat down in a chair and looked at Kevin and Oliver. "I have a proposal." She took a couple seconds to compose her thoughts. "We're supposed to examine Stone's wartime experience, right? How the war impacted him—and vice versa."

"Uh-huh," Oliver said.

"Ollie, had you ever heard of Stone before we chose him for our project?"

"No." He slid the laptop into his backpack.

"But you know a lot about the Civil War."

". . . Yeah . . ."

"Stone is just one of hundreds—maybe thousands—who enlisted, but died before ever fighting. And nobody knows their names. Nobody cares about them."

"Uh-huh—Kevin, start packing that box."

"People don't value their story," Ella said. There it was—that wobble in her voice. "All people care about are battles and generals. Guys like Stone were like . . . like little soldiers in a big war, but their story is just as important."

Oliver nodded. "Right." Why were they still sitting here?

"Little soldier, big war," Kevin said. He snapped his fingers and pointed at Ella. "*Little Soldier, Big War: The*

Forgotten Life and Death of Private Raymond Stone."

Ella nodded. Cleared her throat. Blinked hard. "What do you think of that title, Ollie? It pulls everything together—how Stone gave his life but never fought, and how his story is just as important as any other soldier's."

Deep in his gut, the rebellion rumbled. "It doesn't pull everything together."

"What do you mean?" she asked.

"We're still leaving out Henry Weller, and we don't even know if Stone would have fought in the war without him. That could be an actually cool piece to all this. Not just this Susanna girl."

Ella rolled her eyes.

"And I think the title is confusing," he added, because come on now—that eye-rolling was just not called for. She deserved to hear the truth: that nobody knew about Stone because he didn't do anything worthy of being known.

"What," she asked evenly, "is confusing about it?"

Oliver saw Kevin shake his head slightly. "It's fine," Oliver said. "It's great. Can we go?"

Ella watched him for a second. "Okay. I'll go ask Mrs. Bolton if we can scan the diary and photograph."

"Okay."

She peered at him for another second and then hiked up to the second floor.

"Dude," Kevin said. "Keep it to yourself. If you spill your guts about Stone, you can forget about going out with her. I don't exactly know why, but she's kind of invested in this guy, and I get the feeling that if you insult him or something, she's gonna take it personally."

Oliver felt like the Civil War was about to be fought inside his stomach—a rebellion of Ella's made-up history vs. actual history.

"Got it," he said, slinging his backpack onto his shoulder so hard he almost broke the strap.

-CHAPTER THIRTY-EIGHT-
THE REBELLION OF HISTORICAL ACCURACY

Oliver looked at himself in the giant wall mirror in his parents' bedroom. "I look like a mobster."

"You look great." His dad brushed a piece of lint off the dark suit. "It's a little big, but better than yours. You're growing too fast. We'll have to get you a new suit this summer."

"Where's my handsome son?" his mom called from downstairs.

"Ugh," Oliver said.

His dad turned Oliver around and adjusted the blue tie. "Your first dance. Okay, then. Any questions?"

"Dad."

Oliver's dad held his hands up. "Just trying to keep the door open on the conversation."

Oliver looked at the gigantic suit. The sleeves went almost past his fingertips. "We're not really going together. I mean we are, but just as friends."

"Your mother and I started as friends."

"We've been over this."

"Okay. Well—I think it's great. You went for it. That's the hardest part."

"Come on," Oliver's mom called up. "You don't want to be late for your first date."

"It's not a date," Oliver said.

"Ollie's got a girlfriend," Addie singsonged from the piano room.

His dad clapped him on the shoulder. "Ready?"

"Almost."

Oliver went to the basement to check his email. Nothing from Senior Assistant Amanda DeFrancesca. Of course. Why should anything about this project go his way?

Oliver grabbed his book bag and went back upstairs, his giant suit pants swishing all the way.

"My little boy." His mom sighed as he walked into the kitchen. "You look very dapper."

"I don't know what that means."

"It means handsome." She kept gazing at him.

Addie scuttled in and looked him up and down. She tugged on the long suit coat sleeve. "It's too big."

"I'm aware," Oliver said.

"Why are you bringing your book bag?" his mom asked.

"Uh." He really should have planned out that lie beforehand. "Extra clothes in case I get sweaty. From all the dancing."

She bought it. "Now: the corsage."

Oliver's dad dug something out of the fridge. It looked like a giant pin made of strangled flowers.

"What is that?" Oliver asked.

"It's a corsage." His mom took it out of the plastic container and held it over her heart. "You attach it here, on her dress."

"I have to put that on her?" Oliver asked.

Addie laughed.

"You'd think they'd make them with clasps by now," his mom said. She winked at Oliver's dad. "So nobody can accidentally stick you in the collarbone and get blood all over your dress at senior prom."

"Maybe if somebody's dress wasn't so distracting," his dad said, "I would have had better aim."

"I'm leaving," Oliver said.

"Let me drive you," his mom said.

"I'll walk. I do it every day."

"I don't want you to get your suit dirty." She gave him a side hug. "Let's go."

Oliver sat in the way back of the van. It still kind of smelled like strawberry shortcake. Wendy's lingered in the air too. He was equal parts terrified and excited.

"I think this is great," his mom said.

"Ugh."

"My little boy. Going to a dance. Kinda makes me feel old."

"Mom, are you going to cry?"

"No." She was about to.

The van eased into the school bus loop. Kids were unloading here and there. Oliver wondered why the guys wore shorts and tank tops instead of suits. The girls wore grass skirts and giant flower necklaces like he'd seen on Hawaiian vacation commercials.

"Have a great time, honey."

"Thanks." He got out and shouldered the backpack. His mom took one more look at him and pulled away.

Cars flooded in and more kids wearing Hawaiian gear got out. Clearly he'd missed the theme or something. Oliver felt stupider by the second in his dad's giant mobster suit.

And then he saw her.

And instantly forgot everything else.

"Hi," she said.

"Uh. Hi."

Ella looked more beautiful than anyone Oliver had seen in real life.

She looked like a model. From TV.

That seemed like the only fair way to describe her.

"Ella, you look like a model. From TV."

She smoothed her dress and looked around. "Are people still watching us?"

"They're not watching me."

Her face turned fire-hydrant red. "My sister picked it out. She made me wear it."

"Well, you're wearing it like a freaking model."

"Stop *saying* that—"

"Aloha!" shouted Kevin. He climbed out of his mom's Volvo. He was also wearing shorts, a muscle shirt, and a flower necklace. "You two going to a funeral?"

"I didn't know it was a Hawaiian theme," Ella said.

"At least you're in it together." Kevin eyed Oliver's giant suit. "Shall we?"

"Where's Cindy?" Oliver asked as they walked into school.

"Who?"

"Your date."

"Oh. Her. Yeah—we're not going out anymore."

"Why not?"

"She dumped me, if you must know."

"When?"

"An hour ago. Via a drawing of me and her standing on opposite sides of a chasm that read *goodbye*. It's a long story—one I fully plan on writing one day to get back at her, Taylor Swift style. But right now it's too painful."

"She broke up with you an hour before the dance?" Ella asked. "That's really mean."

"Love is a cruel game, Ella. But if you never play, you'll never win—am I right?"

"You can hang out with us," she said, which Oliver didn't like. Fake date or not, it was his fake date—not Kevin's.

"Thanks, but I've gotta roam. See what's out there. You know?"

"I actually have no idea," Oliver said.

"I'm going to hang out with Cindy's friends and see if one of them will fess up on why she dumped me. Just come and find me when you guys head to the lab."

They strolled into the gym and Kevin branched off toward a clump of girls. Oliver looked around and wondered if the place had been decorated by an army of kindergarteners—a few fake palm trees here, tons of leis covering the circular tables there. In one corner a DJ was messing with sound equipment while a few teachers, including Mr. Carrow, made small talk. Across the gym a photographer was taking pictures of students in front of a fake Hawaiian backdrop.

"Do you mind if we get the picture over with?" Ella asked.

"Huh?"

"Charlie wants me to get a picture."

"Okay."

They shuffled over to the picture booth and got a place in line. The couple in front of the backdrop was basically spooning; the guy was holding her from behind. Oliver suddenly got sweaty. Is that what he was supposed to do?

"What's that?" Ella asked. She pointed to the plastic container holding the flower pin.

"I'm supposed to put this on your dress. It's called a corsage." Oliver took out the thing and just held it. No way he was going to attempt pinning it without explicit permission. And even then he would probably refuse.

"It's pretty," Ella said. She took it from him and attached it to her dress herself. Saved.

"My dad bought it."

They shuffled up in line.

"So what made you change your mind?" he asked.

"About what?"

"The dance. The dress. The picture. It kind of goes against your whole mission, doesn't it? Sticking it to your parents?"

Ella chewed on a nail and watched the couple ahead of them get into a pose. Oliver wondered how she was feeling about their imminent hug session. "Charlie's really into this kind of stuff . . . dresses and looking pretty. I thought maybe . . ."

"Great. Perfect couple. Next," called the photographer. He was looking at them. He was an older guy with thinning hair dressed in a black V-neck and black pants. Oliver smelled sour cologne. "All right, so you're going to stand here," he directed Oliver, "and put your arms around her." He basically put Oliver's hands around Ella's tiny waist, which was horribly awkward because the bare facts were that Oliver's first ever physical contact with a girl was under the direction of this random, weird-cologne-wearing dude. "Good. Stay just like that."

Oliver felt Ella shaking. "Are you okay?"

". . . Hmm huh."

"And hold it . . ." the photographer said. He clicked, but there was no flash. "Oh—hold on. Battery on the flash must be dead. Gotta change it out."

Was Oliver supposed to let go? *Oh jeez.* Who knew these things. Kids were starting to smirk in line.

"You were saying that you thought dressing up would . . . would what?" he asked.

Ella shuddered again. Goose bumps covered her shoulders. ". . . I thought maybe if I was more like her . . . maybe my parents would acknowledge that I exist."

The photographer dropped a battery as he ripped open a fresh pack.

This could be a while.

And also: Ella's hair smelled so good, Oliver wanted everything to smell like that, forever.

"I get it," he said.

"Do you think that's . . . stupid?"

"No."

"Well, I kinda do." She sighed, like she was mad at herself. "And as soon as I stepped out of the car and people started staring, I don't know . . . I felt weird. This isn't me—I'm not pretty like her. And I don't really *want* to be like her, I just want her and them to act like I'm not an extra in their epic movie."

"Uh, I've never seen her, but I can tell you that you're very pretty. Insanely pretty. Unbelievably—"

"I get it." Ella looked down at her dress and huffed. "I wish I'd never come."

"Do you wanna just go to the lab now?"

"Let's get some food first."

"Okay."

"Now give me a big smile," the photographer said. "On three: one, two . . ." The flash went off and blinded Oliver. "Great. Perfect couple. Next."

They wandered over to the buffet and loaded up. Mostly Ella loaded up. By the time they reached an empty table, stuff was falling off her mountain of food.

"I didn't know hot dogs were Hawaiian," Oliver said, eyeing his dinner.

Ella had half of hers in her mouth and mumbled something that sounded liked *hmmmumphphm.* It was actually kind of comical seeing her so dressed up but still eating like a gorilla.

"The power couple." Mr. Carrow rapped the table with his knuckles and sat in an open chair across from them. "So . . . how was it? The big trip to G-burg? Give me the deets."

"Really, really good," Ella said. "We got into the archive and found exactly what we were looking for."

"And?"

Ella smiled with her entire face. "You'll have to wait until Monday."

"Mrs. Mason and I are super pumped to see the final product." Mr. Carrow eyed Oliver. "Finding the Civil War . . . different from what you thought, Ollie?"

Oliver felt the regiments lining up in his gut: the Actual Civil War vs. the Ella version. Rifles were loaded and everybody was just waiting for a commanding officer to shout *fire.*

"It's been interesting," he said. He squashed the follow-up: *It could have been amazingly interesting if we had actually used my ideas.*

"Such as . . . ?"

Oliver shifted. His mobster suit swished. "It's different."

★ *235* ★

"Different how?"

Mr. Carrow was really not going to let him out of this.

"Not as much fighting as I thought."

"And what do you think about that?"

"It's fine."

"You sound disappointed."

"No." *Yes.*

"What do you think of Private Stone? Has he helped you see the war from a different perspective?"

An extremely boring and stupid one that nobody should care about, Oliver thought, and as he thought it, he felt gunfire erupt in his gut. All the tension he'd been holding in exploded in a thunderous volley of shots. Mr. Carrow and Ella were both glaring at him for some reason, but Oliver didn't care.

But what's weird is that he also could have sworn he *heard* himself say it—like the words had come out of his brain, bounced off the metal gym rafters, and echoed around the table for everyone to hear.

And that's when he realized that he did say it.

Out loud.

"It's about time you got that off your chest," Ella said.

And then she threw—actually *threw*—her napkin at him and stormed out, her black heels clicking on the gym floor.

–CHAPTER THIRTY-NINE–
THE APOLOGY (ROUND TWO)

"**Y**ou said it, or you thought it?" Kevin asked.

Oliver leaned against the gym's folded-up bleachers. It felt like bullets were ricocheting around his gut. "I thought that I thought it."

"But you said it."

"Uh-huh."

"Out loud."

"Yeah."

"That explains why I saw her storm out." Kevin shook his head. "Dude—I told you to keep a lid on it until the project was over."

"It slipped out. I didn't mean to actually say it."

"But you did."

"Yeah."

"That is very unfortunate."

Music started pumping from the speakers and the lights dimmed. The disco ball glittered. Some students—mostly sixth graders—had formed into two packs: boys on one side, girls on the other.

"You need to go talk to her," Kevin said. "For the sake of the project."

"I know."

"And you need to apologize. I don't care if you don't mean it. Just do it."

Oliver grabbed his backpack and walked out of the gym. The computer lab was on the other side of the building, so he had to squeeze past a retractable iron blockade meant to keep students from running around unsupervised.

Oliver didn't want to apologize. He wasn't sorry. It actually felt amazing to have it all out in the open. He didn't want to go back to pretending that Private Stone was anything other than a boring soldier who'd pooped himself to death.

Okay, so he would fake-apologize. He'd lie to Ella and then they could get working. They'd still get their hundred. Everything was going to be okay.

The computer lab was dark. Oliver pushed the handle and the door creaked open.

"Ella?"

Empty.

He took out his phone and texted her.

No response.

Oliver wandered back through the iron gate into teacher-chaperoned territory. He passed the bathrooms. He really hoped she wasn't crying in there. Putting his ear to the door, all he heard were toilets flushing.

At the main office he ran into Ian and Samantha. They were holding hands and laughing about something.

"Hey," Oliver said. "Have you seen—?"

Ian made a *yikes* face and pointed outside. In the fading light Oliver saw Ella in her dress standing by the flagpole. She was talking on her phone.

"Good luck, man," Ian said.

Oliver stepped out into the humid night and took off his mobster suit jacket. He probably had major pit stains. He definitely had butt sweat. He loosened his tie and walked over to Ella.

"Please," she pleaded. "Just pick me up." A pause. "Charlie—I tried, okay? Just come get me."

Oliver felt something sitting on his chest—a reverse hero feeling. It was like he'd made her faint this time and then laughed as she crashed to the floor.

"Please," Ella begged. "Charlie, I will walk home—watch me. I don't care that I'm in black and it's almost dark. I—" Pause. She relaxed. "Okay. *Okay.*"

She hung up and wheeled around.

"I'm sorry," Oliver said. "I'm really sorry I said that."

Ella ignored him and walked to the edge of the side-walk and sat on a bench.

He followed.

"I shouldn't have said that, okay? I'm sorry. Don't leave. We can still get a lot of stuff done."

"You're sorry." Ella looked the other way. "Like when you tried to kick me out of our group?"

Oliver's old friend, the fist of guilt, punched his lower intestine. "That was different."

"How?"

"I'm not used to working with other people."

"That's an excuse," she said. "And a bad one."

"But it's true."

"Which should make it all okay, right? Wrong, Ollie. You don't get to use that as a reason to be a jerk."

"You said you forgave me," he said.

"Maybe I did what you do: Say something without actually meaning it."

"What's that supposed to mean?"

Ella slowly turned her head and looked at him. Her Caribbean-blue eyes gleamed. "Stone, Ollie. This *whole* project. We're telling a story about an actual person—but you don't believe he mattered. You've been nodding along with me but you don't actually believe it. Instead you've been faking, all while going off on some weird tangent about the regiment he enlisted in so you can get lost in more of what you really love: details that don't actually matter."

Oliver could hear Kevin screaming in his head.

DO. NOT. SAY. IT.

JUST.

APOLOGIZE.

YOU.

MORON.

But it was too late.

The soldiers had re-formed and reloaded. They were ready—they wanted—to fire again, and Ollie wanted them to.

And so he gave the command.

Fire.

"You're right," he said. "I don't believe it."

Ella stood and took a step toward him. Her pale skin was blotched with rage. "Why—because he wasn't some hero from your Time-Life books?"

"He *wasn't* a hero. All he did was march around, get diarrhea, keep score in the stupid camp baseball games, and die."

"He volunteered to give his life for this country."

"Yeah, in exchange for a ton of money," Oliver said. "Real honorable."

"What are you talking about?"

"Haven't you been listening to me? Stone enlisted in

place of this H. Weller guy and money was exchanged."

Ella pressed her fingers into her temple. "This is exactly what I'm talking about: You're obsessed with every detail but the ones that actually matter."

"*I'm* obsessed? I'm not the one who has a gigantic crush on Stone."

"*I don't have a crush on him!*" Ella shouted. "We were supposed to examine his wartime experience. I'm pretty sure everything in his letters—including falling in love right before he died—qualifies. You're just mad because he didn't match up with your perfect little world of battles and generals. But guess what—that stuff has absolutely zero impact on our project."

"It's not my perfect little world," Oliver yelled back. "It's called *history*—the real history of the war that I know way more about than you."

"Oh right—your big mountain with all the hidden details and information and gold mines that nobody knows but you." Ella glared at him. "You know, Ollie, I seriously wonder if you *really* like the Civil War because there's nobody up on your stupid mountain of facts but you. I wonder if maybe you're up there because it's easier than being down here with the rest of us."

It was like getting punched in the heart. Oliver let his backpack fall to the ground with a *thud.*

Ella must have seen the damage she'd done, because she reached toward him. "Ollie . . ."

But he'd recovered now and was hungry for payback. The ammo wasn't hard to find.

"Says the girl living up in the twin peaks of Mount Bad Grades and Worse Hair. And why are you up there? To send your parents some stupid message about not getting enough attention? 'Cause your sister doesn't wanna hang out with you? Here's an idea: Ever think about actually *talking* to them? If you want to accuse someone of hiding, maybe you should look in a freaking mirror."

Ella opened her mouth; nothing came out. He'd hit a nerve. No—he'd charged into an inner chamber of her heart, bayonet fixed, and stabbed with intent.

A pair of headlights lit up Ella's stony face. A lime-green Volkswagen Beetle pulled into the parking lot and Ella got in.

CHAPTER FORTY

THE TERRIBLE, HORRIBLE, AWFUL, EMBARRASSING TRUTH

"Hey buddy." Mr. Carrow sat down on the curb next to Oliver. "Everything okay?"

Oliver watched the taillights of Charlie's VW Beetle disappear down the road. "Uh-huh."

"Trouble in paradise?"

Oliver picked at the gravel. "I guess."

"I should probably admit that I was getting something from my car just now." He pointed to a red beat-up Honda Civic that looked like it was one fender bender away from the junkyard.

"So you . . . heard all that?"

"Yeah."

They sat in silence for a while.

"I wanna show you something." Mr. Carrow pulled out his phone and did an image search. He clicked on a picture and showed it to Oliver. "Check it out."

Oliver examined a giant bronze statue of a bearded soldier on horseback. The statue sat on a cement pedestal, putting it probably twenty feet in the air. "Looks like a memorial."

"Yup. Now, if you walked by this, what would you think about that guy?"

"I'd think he did something really awesome during the war."

"Something heroic."

"Yeah, I guess."

Mr. Carrow zoomed in on the statue. "Here's the inscription: *Those hoof beats die not upon fame's crimson sod, but will ring through her song and her story; He fought like a Titan and struck like a god, and his dust is our ashes of glory.*"

"Sounds like he did something really cool."

"It does." Mr. Carrow pocketed his phone. "The guy on that horse is Lieutenant General Nathaniel Bedford Forrest, a really famous Confederate commander who did a lot for the South during the war. A very brave soldier. Ever heard of him?"

"His name sounds familiar."

"But from the statue and inscription, he sounds like a hero, right?"

"Yeah." Oliver sensed this was a setup, but his answer was honest.

"In 1864, Nathaniel Bedford Forrest and his cavalry killed over two hundred surrendering Union soldiers—most of them African Americans—at the Battle of Fort Pillow. Historians call it one of the worst massacres of the Civil War."

Oliver stared up at his teacher. "That's horrible."

"Gets worse. After the war, Forrest joined the Ku Klux Klan—the guys who went around in white robes terrorizing and, in many cases, actually killing African Americans who were trying to vote."

Oliver couldn't help but think of Mrs. Mason. "Why does a guy like that get a memorial? He's a murderer."

"Think about this: After the war, white Southerners had to face the fact that they lost—badly. Their countryside was torn up. Almost a third of their male population was gone or maimed. And they didn't want to adjust to the new world order—a society without slavery, and a rush of free African Americans competing for the same jobs as poor whites. How do you think they felt?"

"Sad. And probably angry."

"Exactly. And so they channeled all that sadness and anger into hero making. Historians call this the Lost Cause era—a time when the defeated Confederates focused on celebrating their soldiers' bravery and heroics instead of dealing with the realities of the war—its causes and consequences, including atrocities committed against real people, like the Fort Pillow massacre." He looked at Oliver very seriously. "What I'm saying, Ollie, is that people sometimes make history what they want it to be instead of what it actually was. They focus on the parts that fit with how they feel instead of looking at the big picture."

The statement plunged into Oliver's chest like a bayonet.

But then something strange happened: The blade turned cold, almost soothing. It felt right. It felt like the truth.

The terrible, horrible, awful, embarrassing truth.

"I do that," he said.

Mr. Carrow let that sit for a little. "Part of the reason I didn't want you to work alone is because I wanted you to see the war as it was—not as you made it. Don't get me wrong: I love that you reenact. I love that you know more about the Battle of Gettysburg than probably most of the social studies teachers in Pennsylvania. But there's a big difference between knowing stuff about the Civil War and understanding the human conflict. It's not all battles and generals and heroes. Sometimes it's a local farm boy who enlists, spends a couple months marching around writing letters to his mom, and then dies without ever firing a shot."

Oliver took in a giant lungful of humid air and let it out slowly. "Yeah. I'm getting that now."

"I put you with Ella for another reason too."

"Because I have trouble working with other people," Oliver said. "I'm pretty sure we didn't accomplish that mission."

Mr. Carrow hid a smile. "I was trying to help Ella."

Oliver felt the truth of it dawning on him like a sun—slow at first and then blinding. He'd been too focused on himself to even think about it. Too selfish.

"Because she's got things going on with her," he said. "Because she needed a friend."

Mr. Carrow nudged Oliver. "Don't we all?"

The sound of crickets filled the air for a few seconds. "What am I supposed to do now?" Oliver asked.

Mr. Carrow pulled his face tight. "That's a tough one. You said some pretty harsh stuff; the thing about her hair comes to mind."

"That was bad."

"Very bad. But in my experience, humility mixed with a genuine apology—maybe a grand apology, in your case—can speed up the forgiveness process. Ella doesn't strike me as the kind of girl to hold a grudge."

"Lucky for me, I guess."

"Lucky indeed."

CHAPTER FORTY-ONE

THE APOLOGY
(FOR REAL THIS TIME)

An hour later Oliver was sitting on the couch in his basement staring at his collection of regimental flags. They used to make him feel cool—like a die-hard that was so legit, he'd amassed these super-rare objects.

Now they made him feel a little silly.

Oliver got up and started taking them down. He didn't know what he was going to do with them—not throw them out—but he didn't really want them up anymore.

Kevin texted that he was coming over. Twenty minutes later Oliver let him in and they went back to the basement.

"Some people at school said they saw you and Ella yelling at each other by the flagpole," Kevin said. "I guess things didn't go as planned."

"Not exactly."

"What are you doing?"

"Taking the flags down."

"How come?"

"Just 'cause."

Kevin walked over to the coffee table where Oliver had stacked them and began to fold. "So what happened?"

"She told me something I didn't want to hear and . . . and I said some really mean stuff back. I acted like a giant idiot."

"Did you break up?"

"We weren't going out."

"Right." Kevin ran his hand across one of the flags. "So what are you gonna do?"

"About what?"

"About getting her back so you can finish the project. So I can boost my English grade. So I can accomplish my goal of becoming the first seventh grader in the greater Northeast area to have one thousand Wattpad followers."

"I actually have no idea." Oliver dropped the folded flags on his bed and plopped down on the couch. "Mr. Carrow said I have to apologize."

"For the record, I also said that."

"Yeah, I know. But this time it has to be real. And big. Mr. Carrow said something about being grand. But I've apologized to her before for being an idiot, so I don't know how to make her believe I really mean it this time."

Kevin flopped on the couch arm. "You should serenade her—like in the movies. Go to her window tonight and just start singing this song about how sorry you are. That would be epic."

"And really embarrassing."

"Oh, for sure. Which is why it would work."

Oliver looked at Kevin for a few seconds. Then he looked at the pile of regimental flags on his bed. Then he thought about the electric piano and speaker up in Addie's room.

"Kevin," he said, "how do you feel about waving your arms around and pretending to direct a band?"

"I feel . . . not as weirded out as you might expect. Why?"

Oliver's mind picked up speed. ". . . Sergeant Tom has a snare drum—he brought it to drill this one time . . . I have the regiment colors . . . Addie on piano . . . I think Joe has a bugle or trumpet or something . . . we'll sound pretty bad, but not awful. Or just the right amount of awful. Would be great if we had a microphone or something to make it really loud—"

"Hal might have one," Kevin said. "I'm pretty sure he wants to be a DJ."

"What? How do you know that?"

"Because he runs the historical society's Twitter account. And when he's not retweeting history stuff, he retweets all these DJs you've never heard of and DJ equipment that's supposed to be good. Not super historical, but apparently useful."

"Can you message him or something?"

"First tell me this grand plan you have that involves musical instruments and pretty much every person you know."

"I will." Oliver raced to his desk and fired up the computer. "But first, I need YouTube."

The next morning at eight a.m., the Prichard family van rolled into the nicest development within a fifty-mile radius. Oliver thought each house could hold about five of his houses inside. Maybe six.

"This is it," Oliver said, spotting a driveway with a white Escalade and green VW Beetle. "You can let us out here."

"Do you want me to stay?" his dad asked.

Oliver looked down at the brass buttons on his uniform. "Better not. That way I can't back out."

"I was kind of hoping you'd record it on your phone, Mr. P," Kevin said. "But Ollie's right. There are some things you can't unsee. Or unhear."

"Did you bring extra batteries?" Addie asked.

Oliver patted his book bag. "Yup."

His sister smiled widely. "This is fun."

Oliver wanted to vomit. "Let's go."

They grabbed the essential items from the trunk: the 104th Regiment Flag, Addie's electric keyboard, and the piano stand. Down the street, Oliver spotted Sergeant Tom and Joe getting out of a shiny pickup truck with their instruments. Hauling their gear onto Ella's lawn, Oliver guessed they looked like a lost band of circus musicians.

"Good luck," Oliver's dad said as he pulled away. His grin was a mix of secondhand embarrassment and pride.

"Did you tell Hal the right time?" Oliver asked Kevin.

"Yup."

"We really need that—"

A black Monte Carlo rolled down the street pumping some serious bass. Hal got out of the passenger-side door, unloaded his gear from the trunk, and waved to a person behind the tinted windows.

"Sorry I'm late," he said. "My mom overslept."

"Don't you drive?" Kevin asked.

"I'm only fifteen."

"Seriously? I had you pegged for at least twenty."

"I have one of those older-looking faces. Anyway, I've got your mic and speakers."

"Hal, you rock," Oliver said. He put up his hand for a high five. Hal lightly pressed his hand against Oliver's so they were basically holding hands. He must be new at it too.

Oliver turned to Sergeant Tom and Joe. "Thanks so much. I really appreciate it, guys."

"Are you kidding?" Sergeant Tom asked, shifting the strap on his snare drum. "It's not every day I get to break this baby out."

Joe emptied his spit value. "Where to, Private Prichard?"

"Better get as close as we can," Oliver said as they walked across the lawn up to the gigantic house. "The volume on those portable speakers probably doesn't carry that far."

"She carries," Hal said. "She carries."

"I can guarantee this neighborhood has never had a block party," Kevin said. "This is gonna be epic."

"Here is good." Oliver stopped right in front of a shrubbery walkway, no more than ten feet from the front door. "Okay. Let's do this."

Addie set up her stand and Oliver dropped the keyboard onto it. Hal rigged up the portable speaker cables and did a quick sound check. Sergeant Tom let a few beats fly on his snare; Joe kept at it with the spit value emptying. Oliver unfurled the flag and took up a position in the middle as Kevin did a few practice swipes with a conductor's baton that was really a magician's wand they'd dug out of Addie's costume bin.

The whole routine took less than a minute.

"If this works out," Kevin said, "we should look into doing birthday parties and bar mitzvahs. I mean, we have the gear." He pointed at Oliver with the baton. "Now text her."

Oliver fumbled for his phone and dropped it. He'd been this nervous once before: last night when he was hugging Ella.

Hey. I'm at your house. On the front lawn. Can you come outside? I have something to say. Actually, to sing.

"Did you use my joke?" Kevin asked. "Something to sing?"

"Yeah."

"Nice."

Oliver stared at the phone.

No response.

"You know, I've been meaning to bring something up," Kevin said. "Storyline. Not the project—this one. The storyline of you and Ella. It's a pretty good one."

"Agreed," said Sergeant Tom.

Hal opened some M&M's. Whatever—his job was done.

"Is this really the best time?" Oliver said.

Addie played a few keys. "Ollie says she's not his girlfriend."

"Your brother is in some denial about that," Kevin said.

"Guys, seriously." Oliver's eyes shifted between his phone and the windows, terrified of the moment he'd see Ella peeking out. "Not now."

"I'm just saying that as far as stories go, you and Ella have a great one. Think about it: Two outsiders are partnered together for a project. They each learn that the other is really cool. They become friends. They start to like each other more than friends. They go on an adventure. They have a fight. One of them—you—screws things up majorly. Then you do this grand gesture to fix it." Kevin tried to balance his baton on a finger. "I mean, the only thing left is for you to ride off into the sunset. Which in the modern narrative would be you two making out right here on the front lawn—"

An upstairs window opened, shocking Oliver into a hasty start of his grand apology.

A poorly practiced rendition of "The Battle Hymn of the Republic."

Belting out the Union Army's anthem at eight o'clock on a Sunday morning in full uniform over a sound system arranged by an M&M's-addicted kid while your sister plays the electric keyboard and your only friend randomly waves a baton around and two grown men in full Civil War regalia play drums and bugle is kind of like dropping over the edge of a roller coaster. It was terrifying at first, but once he embraced the terror and let his lungs do their thing, it wasn't really that scary. Oliver had practiced the song about twenty times last night and another ten this morning, and while he didn't exactly hit all the right notes, it didn't matter. No matter what was coming out of his mouth, he was really saying: I'm sorry. I'm really, really sorry. Please forgive me. I'm an idiot. And so on.

Oliver closed his eyes toward the end and almost forgot about being nervous; he was crushing this thing. Yeah, he sounded pretty bad, but that was the point. He didn't care. He *was* sorry. He really *did* want Ella to forgive him. And if this awful, shameful performance took him a half step closer to that, then who freaking cared. It would be worth it.

And just like that, the song was over.

Oliver looked up at the window.

"Ella: I'm so sorry. This time I mean it. I've acted like such a gigantic idiot since we got partnered together, and last night was the culmination of that acting like an idiot. You were right about everything. Stone did matter, even though he didn't fight and died of diarrhea. I just didn't notice soldiers like him before because it didn't really fit with the Civil War I already knew. I got bored, so I found something familiar in the H. Weller thing—which I still think might be something—but I get that it's not part of the project and that the other stuff about Stone's life was just as important. I'm sorry.

"To prove that I really mean it, I wrote an epitaph for Stone's grave, which according to Google, is a phrase or statement in memory of a person who has died. 'Here lies Private Raymond Stone, Beloved Son and Soldier, Who Gave His Life for His Country. A True Hero.'"

Oliver took a deep breath for the finale. "I'm so sorry for everything—from trying to kick you out of the group to last night. And I really mean it."

He squinted up in the morning light. All he could see was her outline.

The window slammed shut.

"You tried to kick her out of the group?" Addie asked. "That's mean."

"Maybe a little repetitive with the 'idiot' stuff," Kevin said. "That's the kind of thing you should have run by me. As Head Writing Consultant, I would have suggested throwing in a couple 'morons' or maybe some adjectives like 'gigantic moronic idiot'—"

"Ollie?" someone called out.

Oliver whirled around.

To see Ella.

Across the street.

And one front yard down.

A white Escalade and green VW Beetle sat in that driveway too.

"You'd think these rich people would diversify their purchases," Kevin said.

Oliver half waved.

"What are you doing?" Ella called out.

"Uh . . . apologizing."

"To who?"

"I thought this was your house." He pointed to the driveway. "The cars—they're the same."

It was hard to read her face from this far back.

"Ollie," Addie said. "I think we should call Dad."

"What—?"

A police SUV rolled down the street and slowed to a stop along the curb—right in Oliver's line of sight to Ella.

"Plot twist," Kevin said. "This is what's called a plot twist."

CHAPTER FORTY-TWO

CAPRI SUN (VARIETY PACK)

"An apology." The tall, thick, very annoyed police officer stared at Oliver, Addie, Kevin, Hal, Sergeant Tom, and Joe as they stood on the edge of the correct lawn. Ella's lawn. By now her parents, Charlie, and about five other families had stumbled out of their houses to see the commotion. "That's very unusual."

"We thought it was our friend's house. I'm really sorry. I can go apologize to that lady." Oliver turned and looked at the forty-something, tight-exercise-pants-wearing woman glaring at him from the front lawn they'd invaded. "Again."

Kevin coughed through a laugh.

"I don't think that's necessary," the cop said.

"I should have double-checked the address, Officer," Oliver's dad said. "It's really my fault."

"She's your friend, and you don't know where she lives?" the policeman asked Oliver.

Oliver cut Ella a quick glance. He didn't know if

she was still mad. Had she heard *any* of the song or the apology? Did almost getting arrested count as a *grand* apology? "We just became friends. For a school project."

The cop turned to Ella's parents. "That true?"

"It is, Officer," Ella's mom said. She sounded really embarrassed, and kept looking around at the gawking neighbors.

"All right." The cop sighed. "Nobody's in trouble here. Just use some common sense next time, okay? People get very protective of their Sunday mornings. They're not so into strange children breaking into song on their front lawns."

"Yeah," Oliver said. "I'm really sorry."

The cop turned to his cruiser. "One last question: Why 'The Battle Hymn of the Republic'?"

"That's a fair question, Officer," Kevin said. "Of all the songs, across all the musical genres, why would we settle with that? I mean, it's like eight verses long."

The cop waited for an answer.

"It's the grandest song I know," Oliver said. "And I needed something grand."

Oliver saw Ella's smile. Everything was going to be okay.

"How about we all have a less grand Sunday, okay?" The officer climbed back into the SUV. "'The Battle

Hymn of the Republic,'" Oliver heard him mutter as he started the car. "You gotta be kidding me."

"Sorry again about all this," Oliver's dad said to Mr. Berry. "Bit of a misunderstanding."

"No harm done," Mr. Berry said, glancing at his phone. "I'd love to invite you in, but"—he pointed at the phone—"conference call."

"On a Sunday morning? You should complain to your boss."

Oliver heard Ella snort.

"Can't," Mr. Berry said, "I am the boss. Okay, well, it was nice meeting you . . ."

"Dave," Oliver's dad said, "Dave Prichard."

"Nice meeting you, Dave. We should get together sometime."

And then things got suddenly awkward. Oliver wasn't really sure what was supposed to happen next. He'd escaped jail, but now he had to finish what he'd started in front of a very live and personal studio audience. Ella's family was all still standing around outside.

Here's to humility, he thought.

"So you're Oliver," Charlie said.

"Uh-huh."

"Kind of a rebel?"

"Uh, sure." He cleared his throat. "How's Hogwarts?"

"What?"

"Your college."

"Wharton," Charlie corrected him. "It's good."

Ella was staring at him.

"Did you know Ella can make a card disappear?"

"I know," Charlie said. "She showed me last night."

"And she can eat a Wendy's meat cube in like a minute."

Charlie threw her eyebrows up and started to walk inside. "I did not know that."

"So," Oliver said. They were finally alone. "What I was trying to say was—"

"I heard you."

"You did?"

"Yeah. I got your text and went to the front door. I watched the whole thing from my house."

"So . . . you heard everything. The song. What I said after."

She nodded.

"Okay, then. Do you . . . forgive me?"

"Yes. It is safe to say that I forgive you."

"Good. 'Cause I'm really sorry. For real this time."

"You made that crystal clear." Giant beaming smile that took up her whole face.

Oliver let out a big sigh. "Okay."

"Okay."

He shifted from foot to foot. "I know that asking about fist-pounding moments takes the momentum out of them, but I actually don't know if this is one."

"It's not."

His stomach dropped. "Oh."

"It's a hugging moment."

And she hugged him.

Kevin caught Oliver's eye and mouthed "More than friends, bro."

Oliver let go first because he wasn't really sure how long you're supposed to hug someone, even if you're pretty sure they like you more than a friend. "We've got some work to do, huh?"

"We do."

"You wanna come over, maybe?"

"Maybe after I eat breakfast. And after I change out of my pajamas. And you change out of your wool pants."

Oliver almost forgot it wasn't even eight thirty. "Right."

"You should have kissed her," Kevin said. They were back in the basement waiting for Ella. Oliver couldn't ever remember feeling better in his life. It was like a sumo wrestler had decided to get off his chest. "One last plot twist, and then the resolution. That's the make-out session. The story would be complete."

"Wouldn't that mess up the group chemistry?"

"I think we've all come to realize you two are very capable of messing things up sans make-out. Besides— the project is pretty much over."

Oliver was actually kind of sad about that. Would he and Ella still see each other? Would he and Kevin? Hal was probably out of the picture.

"What will we do, you and me?" Oliver asked. It was a logical question. The only thing binding them now was Private Stone. "I mean like, when we're hanging out and stuff after all this is over?"

"I assume we'll continue to eat a lot of Cheez-Its," Kevin said. "And I've been meaning to introduce you to Clash of Clans. I know, I know—you don't like video games. But they're supposedly making a Civil War version."

"Cool."

The basement door opened and Ella came down the steps.

"Where'd the flags go?" she asked.

"Took 'em down last night."

"How come?"

"Just felt like it was time."

Ella plopped down next to him and unpacked her laptop and binder. "I figure we don't have much work left. Really just minor changes and tweaks. I say we hook this up to the TV and watch from start to finish, take notes, and then combine our thoughts."

"The Head Writing Consultant agrees," Kevin said.

"Same," Oliver said.

"The Head Writing Consultant is also thirsty, and will return with drinks." Kevin bounded up the steps.

Oliver brought the laptop over to the TV and started finding the right cords. "Think we'll get a hundred percent?"

"Maybe."

"Don't you need a perfect score to pass seventh grade?"

"Not anymore. I completed a bunch of missing assignments last night for some other classes when I got home."

"Really?"

Ella chewed on the inside of her cheek. "Last night you said something that made a lot of sense to me."

"Last night I was a gigantic moronic idiot—"

"Maybe, but you weren't wrong. What you said about my plan—about the message I was trying to send my family by dressing a certain way and failing. You were right: I was hiding too." Ella shook her head. "I didn't realize until last night how exhausting it all was. So . . . thanks, I guess. Thanks for helping me see that."

"I don't really deserve a thank-you."

"Yeah, you do. And an apology. What I said about you hiding up on your Civil War mountain—that was mean. Really mean. As soon as I said it I felt awful. I'm sorry I steamrolled you on your H. Weller thing."

He shrugged. "It's okay. I never heard anything back from the emails anyway."

Ella nodded. "I guess I thought I wanted to find out about Susanna because I really, *really* wanted Stone to matter. I *needed* him to matter." The wobble in her voice was back. "I felt like I was him: a tiny person in a family that cares about big things like money and work and being smart. I felt like nobody cared about my story that wasn't nearly as interesting."

Oliver felt guilt wash over him. "That makes sense."

Ella got off the couch and joined him by the TV. She sat on her knees and looked him in the eye. It was very likely this was a dream. "Thanks, Ollie."

"For what?"

"For the song. For always sticking up for me with my family."

Oliver could hear Kevin yelling in his head.

Kiss.

Her.

NOW.

Was he at the resolution of his own story?

"Coming in hot." Kevin threw something at Oliver as he stomped down the steps. "Oh—*crap*—"

Oliver reached up to grab the flying Capri Sun. It was instinct. Maybe if he'd been an athlete it would have been a more graceful instinct. But Oliver wasn't an athlete. He hated ball sports because he sucked at them.

And because he sucked, Oliver didn't catch the Capri Sun.

It hit him directly in the face.

And he dropped Ella's laptop.

CHAPTER FORTY-THREE

THE ALL DAY/NIGHTER

"Crap crap crap," Kevin said.

Oliver stared at the laptop through one eye. His other one was watering from being hit with a Capri Sun.

Ella tried the power button again.

Nothing.

"Maybe it's just the battery," Oliver said. This couldn't be happening. It just couldn't. Not after all the work they'd done—not after the roller coaster of the last twenty-four hours. "Plug it in."

Ella dug the charger out of her backpack and connected it. The beacon lit up green.

Full battery.

"Crap crap CRAP!" Kevin shouted. "I ruined everything."

"I dropped it," Oliver said, trying to make Kevin feel better.

"Crap crap crap crap," Kevin murmured. He started

pacing around like a possessed robot. "Mother. Freak-ing. CRAP!"

The only person who didn't seem worried was Ella.

In fact, she looked the opposite of worried.

She looked . . . amused.

And now she was laughing.

It was a full body laugh that shook her shoulders and made tears stream down her cheeks. She was laughing so hard, she looked like she was sobbing.

"Ella." Oliver wondered if maybe she was losing it. "Uh. Are you okay?"

She waved him off, wiped tears from her face, and then flopped onto the couch. She calmed down for a second, and then burst out laughing again.

"She's snapped," Kevin said. *"CRAP!"*

"I'm . . . fine . . ." Ella gasped. "I'm fine." She wiped her eyes with the heels of her hands. "Okay. For real this time: I'm fine. It's just unbelievable, isn't it? I mean, after three weeks of research, hours of filming, a trip to Gettysburg . . . this happens."

"I'll pay for it," Oliver promised. "It might take a while, but I've got some birthday money saved up—"

"I don't care about the computer," she said. "It was a Trojan horse anyway."

"A what?"

Ella looked at the laptop like she was glad it had

died a sudden death. "My parents got me this a month ago—said it was an early birthday gift. Six months early." She sighed. "I knew it was a trick because we met with Mrs. Fastbender a week later and they both kept bringing up how they were doing everything they could to help me at home—even buying me my own laptop."

"Oh." But Oliver still didn't see the humor here. Their project was lost. "Maybe Mr. Carrow will give us an extension."

"Not a three-week extension," Kevin said. "It'll take forever to re-create this thing."

Ella stood up and smoothed out her ponytail. She walked to the computer, tried to turn it on again, and finally shut the lid. "No, it won't."

"What?"

"It won't take three weeks. I don't even think it will take more than a day. And maybe a night."

"You think we can redo the *entire* thing for tomorrow?" Oliver said. "That's insane."

"No, it's not." She walked to the butcher paper storyboard still hanging on the wall. "I still have all the raw footage on my iPhone, and my dad has a MacBook Pro I can use to edit. We have Kevin's finished script. We just have to throw it all together. Again."

Kevin had stopped saying *crap* long enough to nod.

"But the editing," Oliver said. "That'll take more than a day."

"No it won't," Ella said. "I've gotten pretty good, and I know exactly where to cut each shot already." Ella looked at both of them. "Guys: We can do this."

Oliver couldn't believe he was actually starting to buy it. But they didn't really have a choice. The thing was due tomorrow.

"Okay." He nodded. "Let's do it."

As soon as Charlie dropped off Ella's dad's laptop, they dove in headfirst. Yeah, there were a few disasters, like when Oliver accidentally clicked on a pop-up spyware ad and they got the spinning wheel of death for twenty minutes before restarting the computer and praising Steve Jobs for iMovie's autosave feature. But then Ella would say something encouraging and Kevin would crack a joke about that time they had to redo an entire project in one day and Oliver would forget the insanity of it all. They were making it happen.

And parts of the documentary got better, like when Ella suggested they reshoot Stone's death in the guest room upstairs because of the lighting. She even starred as Susanna Wentworth to play up the romantic trag- edy angle, and while it murdered Oliver's abs all over again, the performance no longer screamed *This was made by a thirteen-year-old.* Addie pitched in by looking up Civil War sheet music and recording it on her keyboard to save them time during editing. Oliver's mom bussed them sandwiches (and Cheez-Its) to keep up their energy. Capri Suns were not allowed. Oliver's dad drove Ella's laptop all the way into Philly just to see if the Apple tech nerds could get anything off the hard drive. They couldn't.

"Good," Kevin said. "I think we're doing it way better anyway this time."

By dark Ella had trimmed all the footage and was halfway through redoing the title with Kevin. There was nothing for Oliver to do until they finished, so he collapsed onto his bed.

The basement lights were dimmed when he woke up. He could see Ella's face glowing in the light of the computer screen. He heard the rapid clicking of her mouse and he knew she was slaying it.

The clock read *9:38.* He'd slept for almost two hours.

Oliver rubbed his eyes and wandered into the bathroom to drink a gallon of water. Near the couch he almost kicked Kevin, who was sprawled on the floor, drool flowing freely from his mouth, crumpled copies of the script in his hands. Oliver stepped over him and settled in beside Ella.

"How's it going?" Oliver whispered.

Ella took her earbuds out. "Good. Almost done."

He watched her drag and drop some transitions in, rewind to view, and then make some small changes. She was like a Hollywood editor whiz kid. How could he ever have doubted her documentary skills?

"Should we record somewhere else, so we don't wake him?" Oliver asked, nodding at Kevin.

"Nah. He's a deep sleeper. I sneezed three times in a row pretty loud and he didn't move." Ella nodded proudly at the screen. "Okay. I think we're ready for you."

Oliver gently took the script from the out-like-a-bear Kevin and plugged in the laptop mic. He cleared his throat a couple of times and then launched into his lines. It started out pretty rough—lots of false starts, as his brain was still waking up—but soon he got into a rhythm. Every now and again Ella would tell him to redo one, and he didn't argue. She was the director here—she always had been. He'd just been too blind and stubborn to see that she was trying to make pure gold.

He finished just after midnight.

"Fourteen hours and fifty-two minutes," he said. "We redid an entire project in fourteen hours and fifty-two minutes."

"Let's watch it."

Oliver walked the laptop to the TV like it was a packet of dynamite. After hooking everything up, he sat back down on the couch. He wasn't sure if he'd sat closer to Ella, or if she'd scooched closer to him, but they were definitely sitting really close, and neither of them seemed to mind.

"Should we wake the Head Writing Consultant?" Oliver asked.

"No. Just us."

Oliver was down with that.

For the next nine minutes they watched the day's furious work play out on screen. Ella took notes along the way, but Oliver just stared. He was mesmerized. It really *was* good.

No—it was *great.*

When it ended Ella reopened iMovie and fiddled around with tiny changes, then they watched it again. She must have been satisfied, because when the screen went black she just sat there. Her head fell onto Oliver's shoulder.

"We did it."

If Kevin weren't snoring, he'd probably shout for Oliver to *JUST KISS HER ALREADY.*

And Oliver wanted to. He didn't know how to do it, exactly, but he wanted to.

But he didn't need to.

This was enough.

Sitting in the dark with a girl he thought more intricately cool and genuinely beautiful than anyone he'd ever met.

A girl who could do the most amazing card tricks you'd ever seen.

A girl who thought reenacting the Civil War was cool.

A girl who could and would destroy you in a hot-dog-eating contest.

Ella Berry.

The greatest girl he'd ever known.

-CHAPTER FORTY-FOUR-
THE DESCENDANT

"Okay gang, listen up." Mr. Carrow sat on the auditorium stage and waited for the scattered conversations to end. "We're gonna see four documentaries today. You've got your rubrics. Tomorrow we'll be back in my room for a gallery of the exhibits, and then in the lab Thursday to check out the websites and papers." He held up the worksheet. "Score as you see fit, but remember this is not a popularity contest. Be fair. The project with the highest scores will receive a prize so amazing that if I told you what it was, your head would explode."

Oliver saw Ian shoot up his hand.

"There's no prize, is there?" Ian asked.

"The prize is your grade. So, yes, technically there is."

"I'm really nervous," Oliver whispered to Ella. "My face is about to be on a gigantic screen in front of the entire class."

"I like your face."

Oliver decided it was safe to assume they were more than friends. "Should we tell Mr. Carrow we did the whole thing yesterday?"

"No way."

"Deal."

Oliver's stomach got tighter by the minute as they watched the other documentaries. One of them was good; one was okay. The last one was just terrible. In general they all used still photographs instead of footage, and the voiceovers weren't always in sync with the images. Sometimes you couldn't hear them at all because the music was too loud; other times the mic was scratchy. Oliver thought Ella should be a consulting director or something for middle school film projects. She would have caught stuff like that.

"Last one, gang," Mr. Carrow said from the rear of the auditorium. "Bring me your flash drive, Ollie."

Oliver walked back and gave his teacher the memory stick. Based on everything that had happened, he half expected the file to be corrupted, but Mr. Carrow opened it, no problem.

"Just waiting for Mrs. Mason and Kevin to join us," Mr. Carrow said. "Hey. I heard a rumor that some kids almost got arrested yesterday for disturbing the peace in one of the neighborhoods. Something about singing

'The Battle Hymn of the Republic'? Apparently there was a snare drum. You wouldn't know anything about that, would you?"

Oliver hid a smile. "Nope."

The rear auditorium door opened and Kevin bounced in. Mrs. Mason trailed after him with a man wearing a really nice suit. He was tall with dark hair and looked the same age as Oliver's dad.

"Who's that?" Oliver asked as he and Kevin headed to their seats.

"No idea," Kevin said. "He was waiting in the office when we walked by. He chatted with Mason and then tagged along."

Oliver slipped back into his seat as Addie's piano track floated through the auditorium. The lights lowered. His heart pounded.

"I think I'm going to be sick," he mumbled.

Ella grabbed his hand and interlaced their fingers. "There's nothing to do now but watch."

The whole handholding thing made everything a little hazy. The nine-minute documentary seemed to go by in seconds. Suddenly people were clapping a little. The lights went on and everyone was filling out their rubrics. Ian turned around and said something to Oliver about putting it on YouTube.

It was over.

"Another round of applause for all of our documentaries," Mr. Carrow said. The students clapped and whistled. "Now get out of my face and go to lunch."

The trio shuffled out of their row with the rest of the herd. Oliver glanced back and saw Mrs. Mason chatting with Tall Suit Guy.

"I don't want to get anyone's hopes up," Kevin said, "but one day we might look back at this documentary as the moment that catapulted us all into greatness."

Mr. Carrow stopped them at the door. "You all know that I love to exaggerate, but I'm being completely honest when I say that in eight years of teaching I've never seen something of such high quality—historically, dramatically, or cinematographically, if that's even a word. You killed it."

Oliver reached out his fist to pound it, but Ella grabbed his hand.

"Not with teachers," she said. "But good instincts."

"And apparently I'm not the only person who thinks so." Mr. Carrow gave Oliver a look. "We have a special guest who would like to meet you. Come here."

He led them to the back of the auditorium, where Mrs. Mason was standing with Tall Suit Guy. Oliver thought Tall Suit Guy's suit looked even nicer up close. Tucked under his arm were two items: a giant, hulking leather-bound book, and a slim folder that read THE WELLER GROUP.

"Ollie, this is Eugene Weller," Mr. Carrow said. "CEO of the Weller Group, a financial institution that he runs with his brother and sister. He emailed me yesterday and I invited him to come see the presentation."

Oliver blinked at the man. "As in . . . Henry Weller? You're related to him?"

"I am," Eugene answered. "And I believe you know my assistant, Ms. DeFrancesca."

"Yeah. I emailed her."

"You did." Eugene had a really warm smile and kind eyes. "I'm sorry I didn't respond sooner. By the time I'd located the pertinent records it was Sunday, and I just thought I'd reach out to your teacher directly. I hope that was all right."

"Uh, sure." Oliver eyed the two items. "Did you find something?"

Eugene opened the folder and removed a clear protective sleeve with a parchment inside.

"My sister is the family historian," Eugene said. "When I shared your email with her she went right for the family estate papers, and she found a few things."

He turned the protective sleeve and letter toward Oliver.

"You did most of the heavy lifting, so I thought you should get to read it to your teachers and group members."

Oliver's heart pounded. The cursive was a little fainter than he was used to—probably from a hundred and fifty years of not being kept in the right conditions. Hal would have had something to say about that.

"Uh." His voice shook from excitement. Ella leaned in on one side and Kevin the other.

Oliver read aloud.

September 2, 1862
Philadelphia, Pennsylvania

I, Henry Weller, being of sound mind and body, and having a deep and abiding conviction to defend this great Union from our Southern brethren bent on secession, but being also bound to the Peace Testimony sworn to before God and the Society of Friends, do hereby contract Raymond Stone as a voluntary substitute to fight in my stead. Furthermore, I, Henry Weller, hereby testify that I have compensated Raymond Stone for his substitution a fee in the amount of three hundred dollars, and swear that should Raymond Stone fall in battle, or succumb to any death or injury as a result of this substitution that renders him in any way incapable of returning to his previous station in life, that I, Henry Weller, shall provide a yearly recompense to William Stone, father of Raymond, for future services otherwise rendered in the family trade, stated here as farmer.

Henry Weller   *Raymond Stone*

"Holy crap," Oliver murmured. *"Holy. Crap."* He looked up at Mr. Weller. "I was right: Henry Weller couldn't fight because he was a Quaker—the *Peace Testimony.* But he *wanted* to fight, so he hired Stone in his place."

". . . Which is why he enlisted in the 68th and not the 104th," Ella said. Her eyes bulged.

"Exactly!" Oliver bounced up and down on his feet, glowing.

"The Peace Testimony is a cornerstone of the Quaker tradition," Eugene said. "While many in the Society of Friends chose to fight anyway, it appears Henry did not. But in secret—likely out of fear that he would be disowned by the Friends who viewed substitution as equal or worse than actual fighting—he contracted this boy, Raymond Stone."

Oliver nodded. This must be how ball sports people felt when they won a championship or something. Then he looked at the giant leather thing.

"Tell me those are bank records," he said.

Eugene opened the book to a red ribbon bookmark. The pages were stained but readable. He swiveled the item so the trio could see. "Once my sister discovered the contract in our family papers, I had a look at our oldest records back at the bank. One thing about bankers, Oliver—and Quakers, for that matter—is that we keep excellent records. I've bookmarked several entries of this loan ledger for you. See anyone familiar?"

Oliver examined the first noted ledger line.

March 4, 1848 | W. Stone | Loan: $100 | Term: 36 months | Interest: 4% | Purpose: Wheat crop

"Stone's dad was a bank customer." Oliver scanned the others, eyes wide. "That's how Henry met Raymond—because Raymond would go down to the city with his dad."

"It would seem so," Eugene said. "While we may never know how exactly the conversation started, I think it is safe to say we know where."

"This is a YouTube moment if I ever was in one," Kevin whispered.

Oliver was completely buzzing from adrenaline. The

pieces were all falling into place literally in front of him.

Eugene held up the Weller Group folder to Oliver and tapped the company's logo: a red diamond.

"I had the opportunity to reread my great-grandfather's will in the course of this little exploration. It contained two very specific commands: First, Henry stipulated that one-quarter of all the company's future profits be donated to community building projects. That part made some sense to me: He'd amassed immense wealth during his life and wanted to give back. But Henry also instituted this red diamond as the bank's logo, yet left no explanation as to why. I did some research myself and learned that Civil War units often used—"

"Badges," Oliver interrupted. "Unit markers. They sometimes sewed them on their uniforms or caps. You think . . ."

He pulled out his phone and Google-image-searched "68th PA Volunteers unit badge."

"I'm lost," Ella said.

"Remember the clover on my drill uniform?"

"Yeah . . ."

He showed her his phone screen. "The 68th was a part of the First Division, Third Corps. This is Stone's unit's badge."

"A red diamond," she said.

"O. M. G.," Kevin whispered.

"I believe my great-grandfather made Stone's unit badge the bank logo to honor him," Eugene said. "A secret memorial to the soldier who died while Henry lived a long and prosperous life."

The buzzing reached a hum. It was the only sound Oliver heard for a while as he looked between all the pieces of the story fitted neatly into their spots. It was beautiful and complicated and totally complete.

Project done.

Mission accomplished.

Mystery solved.

But wait—no. Something was missing, just a small something. A tiny, empty spot near the center that had bothered him this whole time.

"So did Stone enlist just for the money?" Oliver asked. "Was that his main reason?"

Eugene's smile faded. Reaching into the company folder, he pulled out another plastic sheet with a parchment inside.

The mystery continued.

"That," Eugene said, "is actually the primary reason I came." His voice was low and serious now, his mouth pulled tight. "The final document my sister found was a short letter Raymond's father sent Henry Weller in 1866, three years after Raymond died." He cleared his throat and read. *"Dear Sir: I am in receipt of the recent and generous payment this past August. I gratefully request that all future payments cease; as such you may consider this letter cancelation of the contract made between you and my son, Raymond, on Sept. 2 '62."*

Eugene took a couple seconds, like he was having trouble reading it. Oliver wondered if something more was going on.

"I can no longer accept compensation for Raymond's death, for which I am responsible. Sincerely, William Stone."

And then it really went quiet. Outer space, black hole quiet.

"It wasn't for Raymond . . . it was for his dad. He needed the money to hire someone to work on the farm—to take his place." Oliver saw the last, tiny piece settling into place. "And his dad must've felt guilty because he'd kind of sold Raymond into the army like a mercenary, and it got him killed. He couldn't stand to keep getting the money because it reminded him of what he did."

Eugene nodded slowly. Oliver heard Ella sigh real heavy.

Kevin finally broke the silence. "I would hate to ruin the mood with talk of grades and whatnot," he said, looking at Mr. Carrow and Mrs. Mason. "But I would think uncovering a sixteen-decades-old secret would earn us a perfect score."

The teachers exchanged smirks.

"Kevin," Mrs. Mason said, "I think it is safe to say that you and I will not be spending so much time together anymore."

"Thank God—I mean, thank *you,* Mrs. Mason. Thank *you.*"

Mr. Carrow turned to Oliver. "Couple days ago I asked if Stone helped you see the war differently. Got another answer?"

Oliver cut a glance at Ella.

"I used to think the war was a giant mountain with all these details. But now I think the mountains are actually the people who fought in it—like they're the major features and I was down in the valley with all the battle information. Which I guess means the whole thing is even more gigantic than I thought."

Ella looked at him seriously. "Just think what else we could find."

Then she held out her fist.

Oliver stared at the sky as he lay on his back. It was pure blue except for a wispy cloud. He wondered how many soldiers at the Battle of Gettysburg had stared at this same sky right before they died. It was supposedly pretty sunny during the three days of epic carnage, so the answer was probably a lot. The temperature this week ended up historically inaccurate too, thanks to a cold front. All in all, it was a pretty nice day to die.

He craned his neck to look up the wooded hill they'd just charged down. It had been pretty glorious, as far as fake battles go, what with the cannon and gunfire. The 104th Pennsylvania Volunteers and other companies had saved the Union Army from getting outflanked by charging down Little Round Top and sending the Confederate forces fleeing. But Oliver and most of his regiment had made the ultimate sacrifice. Now the only thing left to do was enjoy the view.

Oliver's phone buzzed. He fished it out of his wool trousers and read a text from Kevin.

I think I saw you go down. R u by the big rock?

Oliver looked around.

No.

Oh. Where??? Wave.

I can't wave. I'm supposed to be dead.

OK OK. I'll wave. We're on the dirt road halfway up the hill.

Oliver craned his neck to get a better view of the long line of people snaking up Little Round Top. Kevin was easy to spot in the neon-orange shirt his mom had made him pack so he wouldn't get lost in the crowd. Not exactly historically accurate. He was also jumping up and down and waving. Oliver's parents and Addie were standing behind him.

I see you, Oliver typed.

Cool. OK. When's this thing over? We're supposed to be there by six.

It's over when the battlefield guide—

A man's voice carried down the mountain via megaphone. "Attention reenactors and spectators of the Battle of Little Round Top: This concludes the engagement." The countryside roared with applause. "At this time, stretcher bearers and nurses will attend to the wounded."

A horse-drawn ambulance trundled by. "You wounded?" asked the driver.

"Dead," Oliver said.

"Oh. Okay." He made a clicking noise with his mouth, and the wagon creaked on.

Oliver heard footsteps and turned his head to see a battlefield nurse making straight for him. She wore a white smock over a faded blue, nineteenth-century dress that went down to her ankles, and her hair was pulled up into a bun on the top of her head.

"You're too late," he said. "I'm already dead."

Ella knelt down and unpacked some bandages. "Where are you shot?"

Oliver looked over himself. "Chest, I guess. They didn't really tell us a specific spot. Just that we had to go down."

"Let me see what I can do." She took out a Ziploc bag of Cheez-Its and two Capri Suns. "This is an age-old remedy. Plus, I'm hungry."

"Shocking."

She flicked him. They'd been doing a lot of that lately—flirting. Or Oliver guessed it was flirting.

He looked at her. "Are we going out? I don't have a good record of clarity on these things."

"Oh yeah," she said. "We're going out. Is that okay?"

"Totally."

That was helpful, because with the sun flecking off her face and strands of her brown hair blowing in the breeze, Oliver really wanted to kiss her. Was it inappropriate to make out on a sacred battlefield?

Who knew these things.

His phone buzzed.

Kevin.

KISS HERRRRRRRRRR.

"They had phones in the Civil War?" Ella said.

"Yeah," Oliver said, "but they were only given to the most elite soldiers."

She threw a Cheez-It at him. Then she plopped down beside him to stare at the blue sky. "This was fun. I'm glad I did this."

"Really? I was kinda worried you'd regret it once we got here. It's not everybody's thing."

"It probably helped that I stayed with your parents and Addie at the hotel instead of in a tent with you and Kevin," Ella said. "And that I didn't have to wear one of those giant hoop skirts. Or a corset. It was all really fun."

"Good."

"Did you make up your mind yet about reenlisting?"

"I think I'm done. Maybe not forever, but for now. I've actually been thinking about volunteering at the historical society. Hal could use the help."

"You should try to get him to eat something other than M&M's."

They watched some birds overhead for a while. Oliver's heart did a double beat when Ella grabbed his hand. She was like an inch away from his face. Was this *the* moment?

Oliver jumped as the siren blared.

"That concludes the event," the battlefield guide announced. "We would like to thank our reenactors for putting on such a great show." Thundering applause. "I would like to remind everyone that while the battle is over, our living history tents are still open and excited to usher you into the past. How about another round of applause for our reenactors."

Oliver looked at Ella; she grinned awkwardly and darted her eyes to something else.

Oliver's phone buzzed.

Kevin.

Were you guys just making out?

No.

Oh. You should have been. I'm on my way down. Wave or something.

Oliver waved and the bright orange blur bolted down the dirt road through the tall grass, jumping over several still-dead soldiers.

"Could've used you in the battle," Oliver said to a panting Kevin. "You gonna be able to keep up?"

Kevin wheezed and gave a thumbs-up.

"Then it's time to do what we came here for," Oliver said.

They strolled along a creek bed before hitting a paved road packed with tourists and reenactors. Ella pointed at a field off to the right that rose toward town.

"That's Cemetery Ridge," she said. "Right here is where Pickett's Charge happened. Thousands of Confederates marched through this field at the center of the Union line. It was General Lee's grand plan to break through and win the battle. Instead it was a bloodbath."

"You're really embracing your new hobby," Kevin said.

"The cable was out at the hotel last night," Ella said.

Oliver grinned at her display of knowledge. "When the attack failed, Pickett straggled back with barely half of his men," he said. "General Lee asked him how his division was, and Pickett supposedly said, 'General Lee, I have no division.'"

"Maybe he shouldn't have marched through a mile of open field under heavy artillery fire and then attacked an enemy entrenched behind a fortified stone wall," Kevin said. "But what do I know? I'm not a West Point graduate."

They veered off the road and then trudged up the gradual incline. "I think being here is important," Ella said. "I think I get why people are so obsessed with the Civil War now, especially battles like this one. The scale of danger and death kind of demands respect."

They walked in silence for a while.

"Down here," Ella said, looking between her unfolded map and the road they'd just stumbled onto.

They trailed down Emmetsburg Road and stopped in front of a marble obelisk rising about twelve feet into the air. Oliver thought it looked like a miniature version of the Washington Monument, except this one had a diamond indent in the center: It was the monument to the 68th Pennsylvania Volunteers.

"Looks bigger than the website picture," Kevin said.

They walked around the pediment and read the lone inscription on the far side.

"*In memory of 188 of our comrades who fell on this field July 2nd and 3rd, 1863,*" Ella read.

Oliver stepped back to take in the monument and fields and wooded groves. "And in memory of all those who never got to see it," he said. He took a red diamond patch that he'd bought at the gift shop yesterday out of his pocket and set it down below the inscription. "The other Private Stones."

They gave the monument a few more moments of silence before nodding at one another that it was time to go.

-AUTHOR'S NOTE-

This is a work of fiction but contains a ton of very nonfictional elements. Allow me to clear up some things so I don't anger Civil War diehards, professors, archivists, museum people, and especially reenactors.

PENNSYLVANIA'S VOLUNTEER REGIMENTS

I've taken some creative liberties with the battle actions and muster dates of the Pennsylvania regiments featured in this book. The 104th formed in September of 1861 in Doylestown, and the 68th roughly a year later in Philadelphia. Both regiments fought at Gettysburg; the 68th actually has two monuments on the battlefield, including the one the trio visits at the book's end. Go 68th.

PRIVATE RAYMOND STONE

Private Stone did not exist—or at least not to my knowledge. Who knows: There could be a Private Stone out there somewhere; the name isn't that odd. I googled it just to be sure and came up empty. My point is that I made his name up.

But I based Stone on many soldiers, North and South, using their letters as a guide for syntax and content. For every three soldiers killed in a Civil War battle, five more died of disease. Consider how horrific that is. No really—think about that. Your chances of dying from just sitting around camp—primarily from disease—were basically double the odds of dying in combat.

HISTORICAL SOCIETIES

These places are massive troves of all sorts of amazing historical gems. The local historical society in this book is based on the real Doylestown Historical Society near my hometown, with some details changed to fit the narrative. Ditto for the Adams County Historical Society, located near the Gettysburg battlefields.

GETTYSBURG

Having toured this battlefield as a kid and an adult, I highly recommend a visit. The museums and tours are second to none; these guides know more about the events of that day than Wikipedia could ever hope to. While I don't claim the same, I have attempted to cite all geography, battle details, and monuments with accuracy, and took only slight liberties with the topography.

REENACTORS

I am not a reenactor—Civil War or otherwise—but I have a special place in my heart for the bunch, and have brought them into my classroom to speak. These guys (they are mostly men, but a great many women join their ranks also) take great pride in wearing authentic uniforms, carrying replica weapons, and doing mock battle according to nineteenth-century standards. I have serious respect for their dedication and believe they give the modern observer an accurate window into the past.

The Gettysburg Anniversary Committee runs and organizes annual reenactments, including the especially epic 2013 event to celebrate the 150th anniversary of the Battle of Gettysburg that Oliver and Ella took part in. The real-life event did not feature the Battle of Little Round Top, but the regiments did camp out for several days and wear wool trousers.

QUAKERS AND THE AMERICAN CIVIL WAR

As pacifists, Quakers faced a conflict of conscience during the American Civil War—especially when drafted into service. Some paid the $300 commutation fee, while others abandoned the Peace Testimony and enlisted (mainly in the Union Army). While I have no evidence that a wealthy Philadelphia banker bucked the Quaker tradition to hire a substitute in secret out of grand patriotism, it certainly is not that far outside the bounds of recorded history. I also just thought it was cool.

-ACKNOWLEDGMENTS-

B ooks are like skyscrapers; nobody can build one alone. Here's some people who helped me put this thing together:

Kristy Landis, the wise and beautiful woman who let me put a ring on it and gave us two hilarious kids who have all of my drama and all of her quirkiness. You are my sounding board and cheerleader and the person who says, "Let's take it down a notch, diva" when needed—which is pretty much every five seconds. Most importantly, you remind me that writing is something I do, not someone I am.

My mom, Mary Landis, who first read my really crappy ramblings in high school and told me that I had sort of a way with words. And my dad, Dave, who served not only as the real-life version of Oliver's dad, but whose own love of the history and the Civil War first hooked me. I love you both and would not be writing this now without your support.

Lauren Galit, my amazing agent, who first suggested I write this book because I literally live it every day in my classroom. Incredible work negotiating the tight-rope deal that landed Oliver at Dial; also, incredible work responding to all my emails within forty seconds.

Dana Chidiac, my deeply insightful editor, who fell in

love with Oliver and then fought to get him. Your ability to keep all the pieces of the Stone mystery straight and orient the plot for maximum tension was incredible. I cannot wait for the books we're going to write.

The amazing and hilarious Dr. Judith Giesberg, my Villanova professor, who read an early draft and pointed me to some great sources. Thanks for reigniting my love of the Civil War era, and also for forcing the entire class to be a part of the Emilie Davis diary transcription project, which scarred me for life but also inspired how my characters view cursive.

Team Dial, including Lauri Hornik and Namrata Tripathi, who weighed in on some of the issues of race and history that the book explores; Regina Castillo, for her copyediting skills; cover designers Maria Fazio and Kristen Smith, who accomplished the amazing task of making a book with the word "boring" in the title look anything but; and Mina Chung, who picked amazing fonts and typefaces that even my uber-picky self could live with.

My gracious sensitivity readers, Nic Stone and Cecile Kim, who offered insight into Mrs. Mason and Kevin, respectively.

And God, because I believe He wove this passion for writing into my DNA and put the amazing people above in my life.